RESISTING THE COUGAR

(Cascade Shifters #3)

Jessie Donovan

This book is a work of fiction. Names, characters, places, and incidents are either the product of the writer's imagination or are used fictitiously, and any resemblance to actual persons, living or dead, business establishments, events, or locales is entirely coincidental.

Resisting the Cougar
Copyright © 2015 Laura Hoak-Kagey
Mythical Lake Press, LLC
First Paperback Edition

Cover Art by Clarissa Yeo of Yocla Designs.

ISBN 13: 978-1942211457

To all of my nephews and niece

Without them, my child characters would be a lot less awesome

Other Books by Jessie Donovan

Stonefire Dragons
Sacrificed to the Dragon
Seducing the Dragon
Revealing the Dragons
Healed by the Dragon
Reawakening the Dragon
Loved by the Dragon
Surrendering to the Dragon
Cured by the Dragon

Lochguard Highland Dragons
The Dragon's Dilemma
The Dragon Guardian
The Dragon's Heart

Asylums for Magical Threats
Blaze of Secrets
Frozen Desires
Shadow of Temptation
Flare of Promise

Cascade Shifters
Convincing the Cougar
Reclaiming the Wolf
Cougar's First Christmas
Resisting the Cougar

CHAPTER ONE

Claire Davis adjusted the glasses on her nose and tried not to think about how she was lost in the middle of the cougar-shifters' land. Not lost in the sense she could stop at a gas station and ask for directions. Rather, she was lost in the middle of the damn Cascade Mountains with no cell service and no map.

So much for technology making life easier; it always failed when Claire needed it the most.

Pulling over to the side of the road, she put the car in park and laid her forehead on the steering wheel. If only she had thought of a back-up plan. Reading the directions earlier had made everything seem so simple. What she hadn't accounted for was the low-level fog a few miles back.

Think, Davis, think. She wasn't the head of the Shifter Equality Alliance by luck. Stubbornness was her middle name, and she wasn't about to give up. Especially since her upcoming meeting was important. No, scratch that, the scheduled meeting with the cougar-shifters was goddamn historical.

Kian Murray had invited her to DarkStalker's land through a human acquaintance they shared. Because it was illegal for her, or any human, to be on any shifter's land without the federal government's permission, she'd been given detailed directions to help hide her true destination. Once she reached the final location in the directions, a DarkStalker sentry, named Aidan Scott, would blindfold her and take her the rest of the way.

She'd made it to step number forty-three out of forty-five before the fog had prevented her from finding her next landmark. So close, yet so far.

The number of steps jogged her memory. Raising her head, she then switched on the interior car light and picked up her printed directions. Scanning the page, she reached the end. "Aha. I was right. I'm only a few miles from the final destination. Maybe if I honk my horn and sit here, the cougar-shifters will find me."

Since she was alone on a tiny mountain road, the noise wouldn't attract any humans. Only a fool would try driving these mountains in March with snow still on the ground.

Well, a fool or a woman on a mission. The Shifter Equality Alliance, or SEA, needed this meeting. Without the shifters' help, SEA's push to make shifter-human marriages legal was doomed according to every set of data analyzed in the last few months. Clan DarkStalker was her best chance at making that happen. She needed to make the meeting, at any cost.

Taking a deep breath, she pressed the horn and held it for fifteen seconds before releasing it.

Claire scanned her surroundings, but five minutes later, she was still sitting in her car with no cougar in sight.

If at first you don't succeed, try, try again. The saying might be childish, but it pretty much described how she'd run her life over the last five years.

Placing her hand on the horn, she geared herself for the noise and pressed down. Rather than make it a straight noise, she beeped the horn to "Row, Row, Row Your Boat." Maybe the kids' song would signal she wasn't a threat.

As she waited in silence again, she kept a look out for any cougars. Eventually, they had to find her.

Right?

She refused to think about the alternative.

~ ~ ~

Aidan Scott swished his tail as he paced back and forth in his cougar form, the snow crunching under his paws.

The human was late.

If it were up to him, he'd wait five more minutes and then return home. Humans were certainly not worth his paws freezing in the late season snow. Just because his animal-half could survive in the cold didn't mean he enjoyed it.

However, his clan leader, Kian, had chosen him for this special assignment and he would do anything for the alpha of the DarkStalker cougar-shifters. After all, Kian had been there when Aidan had needed him the most. Aidan wasn't about to repay the debt by abandoning his leader because of Aidan's own prejudice.

If his leader said the meeting with the human female was important, he would treat it as such. He only hoped the human wouldn't betray them. From his experience, they tended to be good at doing exactly that.

A loud noise echoed through the forest and he pushed aside everything to focus. Scanning from left to right, he didn't see anything in the trees apart from the other animals. If there was a threat, it wasn't immediate.

He was fairly certain the noise had been a car horn honking in the distance. Since no one stumbled into these mountains by accident or bothered to look for the best backcountry hikes during early spring, the sound was either the human female or one of the anti-shifter extremist groups.

Given that Clan DarkStalker was hiding a human female named Lauren on their lands, it could just as easily be the latter as the former. He needed to assess the possible threat.

Aidan picked his way through the forest, careful to keep to the shadows and the branches of the trees. Thanks to his tan hide blending in with the trees, no one on the ground would know he was there.

He was nearly to the single-lane road that wound through this section of the mountains when the horn blared again in some kind of rhythm. Thanks to his supersensitive hearing, the sound sent shivers of pain down his spine. It took everything he had to stay on the branch under his feet. The noisy intruder had to be on the road.

Reaching the edge of the woods, he surveyed the area to look for the car. However, a low-level fog had rolled in and he couldn't see anything more than a foot in front of his face.

Fucking fantastic. He'd have to go in blind.

Well, I've been meaning to brush up on my hunting skills anyway. I'll use this as an opportunity. I just hope the person doesn't run me over.

Aidan had no desire to be road kill.

After crawling down the tree, he kept his body low to the ground as he approached the road. No car headlights beamed nearby, nor did he hear an engine running. *Good.* That would make his plan easier.

Inch by inch, he crawled until he could smell the still-warm oil of a car engine. Two more feet, and he could make out the shape of a dark SUV. Shifting his weight, Aidan jumped to the roof of the car. Someone screeched inside. Every cell in his body itched to attack and protect the clan, but if the human female was inside the car, his clan leader would never forgive him.

He moved his head and peered inside the driver's side window. A brown-haired, plump female with glasses was leaning over her steering wheel, no doubt looking for something in the fog.

Since her description matched the female named Claire Davis in his assignment brief, he tapped his claws against the window. The human turned her green eyes to his face.

To her credit, she didn't scream or shout. Rather, her brows came together. She looked irritated.

As if she had the right to be irritated. She was the one who'd gotten herself lost and scared every creature in a five-mile radius.

Jumping off the roof of the SUV, Aidan decided enough was enough. He needed to shift, guide the human to his leader, and then move on to something better worth his time. Concentrating, he imagined his body changing shape.

~ ~ ~

Claire's heart was still beating a million times a minute as the amber-eyed cougar jumped down from the roof of her car. To say the big cat had scared her was an understatement.

However, as the cougar's paws became hands, his face changed into that of a human male, and his tail disappeared into his back, her brain blanked at the tall, naked, and very muscular man standing outside her car window.

Darting her eyes down, she confirmed that yes, he was indeed naked. Even in the cold, the rumor about shifters and their cock sizes seemed to be true.

Stop thinking about the shifter's cock. She wasn't a naïve shifter groupie; Claire knew full well how nakedness was dismissed without a second thought among shifter clans.

With one last long look of his chiseled abs and light spattering of dark and gray hairs on his chest, she met the shifter's eyes. In human form, they weren't amber but brown, and currently filled with irritation.

Flipping the key in the ignition once, she rolled down the window. "Hello. Are you Aidan Scott?"

The man growled. "That's all you have to say? You've been creating a damn ruckus for the last fifteen minutes. The animals in the woods must be terrified."

Remember, you need him to guide you to DarkStalker's land. Be nice to him. "Sorry, I was lost."

He grunted. Just her luck she'd be assigned a grumpy-ass shifter.

Thirty seconds ticked by in silence. The man didn't so much as shiver in the cold.

If the muscles and sneak attack hadn't already proven he was a soldier, the shifter's ability to withstand any circumstance without blinking an eye would've done it.

Another thirty seconds ticked by. She tapped a finger against the steering wheel. If he wasn't going to talk, then she would. "I apologized. If you're waiting for me to beg for your forgiveness, that's not going to happen, buddy."

As soon as the words left her mouth, Claire wished she could take them back.

She opened her mouth to try to soothe the situation, but the shifter male beat her to it. "I don't have time for your chatter. Grab your stuff and follow me."

The shifter male turned and walked away. After a quick glance to his round, firm ass, Claire scrambled to roll up the window. Picking up her duffel bag from the passenger seat, she climbed out of the car and locked it. The shifter was already more

14

than fifteen-feet away. She muttered, "Slow down and give a girl a chance," as she half-ran to his side. By the time she reached him, she was a little out of breath. Fighting for shifter equality didn't leave a lot of time for exercise.

The shifter, who still hadn't confirmed he was Aidan, said, "We've wasted too much time with your antics. Try to keep up."

As their feet crunched in the snow of the woods, she eyed his bare feet. The cold had to be painful.

Normally, she'd hold back and be polite. Hell, how many politicians had she met in Olympia and convinced to support her cause? She could be proper and dignified if she tried. But considering the shifter male was walking stark naked next to her, she figured formalities were out the window. Before she could convince herself otherwise, she asked, "Are you really going to walk how ever many miles naked in the snow? Won't you catch a cold or pneumonia or something?"

Aidan's brown eyes glanced to her and then back in front of them. "I don't need your concern. I know what I'm doing."

She managed to keep her mouth shut. If the man wanted to freeze to death, then that was his prerogative.

Claire, however, dug out her gloves and put up the hood of her winter jacket. Rather than suffer the cold in silence, she tried talking again. "Even if you have super-shifter body heat and don't have to worry about pneumonia, I do. Please tell me there's a car nearby."

"You're the one who got lost. Both of us suffering in the cold is your fault."

She blinked. After so many years of dealing with passive-aggressive behavior in Seattle, Claire wasn't sure of how to deal with Aidan's straightforwardness.

Before she could think of a witty reply, Aidan stated, "I'm going to shift and guide you to where the car is. Stay quiet, just in case."

"In case of what? No one comes up here in March apart from shifters."

He finally turned his head to meet her eyes. "I've lived here my whole life and I know what I'm doing, so listen for once."

"For once? When have I—"

Aidan's shift stalled her words. Watching the process of a man's body shrink into one of a two-hundred pound cougar was something she had always wanted to see, ever since she was a little girl. The morphing of his head into a feline's skull, the tail coming from his back, and his hands and feet turning into paws was beautiful but had to be painful.

Maybe someday she would be able to ask if shifting hurt or not.

Aidan's amber cougar eyes met hers before he motioned with his head and started walking. As the male cougar tracked lightly through the snow, Claire rubbed her hands together and picked up her pace. If she didn't make the meeting with Kian Murray, she would definitely never have the chance to ask a shifter questions about their shifting process. As much as she didn't like Aidan's attitude, she followed his orders and walked in silence.

CHAPTER TWO

By the time they reached the car, Aidan had managed to exercise away the chill. Walking as long as he had while naked had nearly frozen his balls off, yet for some reason, he hadn't wanted the human to know she was right.

Claire Davis was so sure of herself, even when standing up to a shifter, which was rare for humans. Or, at least, most of the humans he'd met in his lifetime. Everyone said Lauren, the pregnant human mate of Sean Fisher, was as fierce as any alpha shifter, but he'd kept his distance. Seeing anyone fierce and in love only reminded Aidan of what he'd lost.

And since he was nearing forty years old, his list of single friends grew shorter by the year. Even his old leader, Sylas, had found himself a mate.

Everyone was destined to find love and keep it, except for Aidan. A day didn't go by when he didn't think of his dead mate. She had stood up to him when few other females dared. They'd fought often and loved even harder afterward. Her flashing brown eyes were a memory that faded each passing year, but he refused to let go. If not for their surviving cub, Aidan probably would've returned to a life of drinking and fighting.

Thinking of his daughter, Chloe, he gave his tail an extra swish and focused back on his mission. The urge to hug his baby girl was overwhelming, but he couldn't do it until the human was safely with Kian.

Keeping a brisk pace, Aidan guided the human through the forest. Soon they reached the thickest part in the area and he stopped. Once Claire stomped up to his side, she glared down at him. "Nice of you to finally allow me to catch up."

Since he was in his cat form, Aidan merely tilted his head and then motioned toward the forest. The human's eyes darted to the dense trees and underbrush before looking back at him. "If we're going in there, you're going to allow me to hold your tail so I don't get lost."

He pulled back his lips to bare his fangs and growl. Rather than frighten the human, she looked bored. "I know your assignment is to bring me to Kian Murray, so growl all you like because I'm not going anywhere unless I can hold your tail."

Great. The human had sass and a brain. That wasn't a good combination.

Do whatever it takes to finish the mission, Aidan. No one is around to see the human grasping your tail.

As a precaution, he studied his surroundings for another minute to ensure they were alone. Satisfied there was nothing but wildlife nearby, he bumped his tail against the human's stomach. After repeating the motion, she lightly wrapped her fingers around his tail. "Your fur isn't as soft as I thought it would be."

He growled and then moved toward the thick foliage. The human must be on a mission to insult him. He only hoped Kian knew what he was doing with Claire Davis. Maybe Aidan should volunteer to watch over her during the meeting. If she disrespected Aidan's clan leader, he would make the female understand that wasn't allowed.

RESISTING THE COUGAR

Resisting a frown, Aidan wondered where the hell that thought had come from. He didn't need to stick around to suffer her insults or attitude. Someone else could watch over her.

As the female stroked his tail, Aidan clenched his jaw and picked up his pace. If word ever got out about a human playing with his tail, he'd never hear the end of it, especially since it had been a long time since a female had brushed her fingers against his fur. If he wasn't careful, he might start to enjoy Claire's soft touch.

No. The only touch he should ever enjoy was his former mate's. To allow anyone else such intimate privileges would violate his mate's memory.

Aidan increased his trot. The car wasn't far. Once they reached it, he could blindfold the female, turn up the stereo, and ride the rest of the way home in silence.

Of course, the human was probably stubborn enough to yell over the music. The image of the female yelling while blindfolded nearly made him smile. Not that he would ever admit to it.

Forcing his face into a badass expression, Aidan guided Claire through the woods and toward the car. He may never take a mate again, but once he dropped off the human, he needed to find a female to ease his tension. His inner cougar's need for sex was messing with his brain. There was no other explanation for why Aidan suddenly wanted the human to pet much more than his tail.

~~~

Claire couldn't resist stroking the fur under her fingertips. Sure, the fur wasn't as soft as a domestic kitten's, but it wasn't too rough, either. Since this was her first time touching a real-life shifter while in animal form, she wasn't going to complain.

Aidan moved and she tried to keep pace. Dodging the trees and undergrowth were difficult and made her glad she'd worn sensible boots and jeans instead of the slacks and dress shoes her coworkers had suggested.

Claire might have lived in a city just south of Seattle for the last five years, but she'd been born and raised in Western Washington State and loved hiking. Only an idiot would hike in heels.

Well, at least an idiot by Claire's standards.

No doubt, Kian would understand. If he turned her away for not showing up in a pants suit, then he wasn't the type of shifter she could see her organization working with. As desperate as she was to gain DarkStalker's support, Claire wasn't about to beg anyone's forgiveness to make it work. After all, she fought for equal standing. She wouldn't be intimidated by a shifter.

Another two minutes, and they broke through the dense forest into a clearing. Sitting in the middle of it was a little black car.

The cougar stopped, turned, and tugged his tail. After releasing it, the cougar grew into the shape of a man again. Careful not to glance down, Claire asked, "Do I want to know where you kept the keys?"

Rather than answer her, Aidan went over to a tree, reached up, and retrieved a small bundle of clothes. She resisted tapping a foot as the shifter dressed. While she'd experienced her fair share of people ignoring her over the years, for some reason Aidan's silence irritated her more than usual. After all, she'd just stroked the fur of his tail. In shifter circles, that was nearly as intimate as a body-to-body hug.

Resisting the Cougar

Aidan pulled out a set of keys from his jeans pocket and glanced at her. "If you want a ride, then hurry up and get in."

Unlocking the car, he slid into the driver's seat before Claire could so much as move a toe. Judging by his behavior, Aidan Scott was used to giving orders and being followed without question. If he were human instead of shifter, she would resist him on purpose just to rile him up. In her experience, male egos needed poking every once in a while.

However, garnering any kind of shifter support was difficult, let alone an entire clan's, so she half-ran to the passenger's side. The engine was already running by the time she clicked her seatbelt. Looking over at the shifter, he held up a pink sleep mask. "Put this on."

She raised an eyebrow. "Is that really necessary? Considering we trekked through the wild forest just to reach your car, I have no idea where we are right now."

"You might once we reach the road. Now, put it on or I leave you here and you can find your own way back."

She stared but the shifter never flinched. With a sigh, Claire took the mask. "Why does it have to be pink? I hate pink."

She swore she saw the shifter's lips twitch. "Just put it on."

"Fine." She removed her glasses, took out the case from her jacket pocket, and slipped them inside. After sliding the pink mask over her eyes, she made a show of feeling around to get her bearings. In the process, she touched the shifter's forearm. The feel of his hair and warm skin against her fingertips sent a small burst of heat through her body.

What the hell? She'd never had that happen before. It must just be her excitement at being on a shifter clan's land.

Realizing she still had her hand on the shifter's arm, she pulled it away. "Sorry. But with this mask, I can't really see anything."

The shifter grunted before turning on the radio. As he turned up the volume, she guessed he planned to spend the rest of the ride listening to blaring music. Too bad she wasn't about to allow him. Reaching in front of her, she touched the glove box, moved her hand over until she felt the knob of the stereo and pushed it. The alternative rock music ceased playing.

Aidan pushed away her hand. "Don't mess with my stereo."

He turned it on again. Claire was about to turn it off and tell him what she thought of the loud, grating music when Aidan captured her fingers with his own. He yelled over the music. "Touch it again, and I will tie you up and toss you into the back seat."

She felt silly yelling, but did it anyway. "Then at least turn it down. It's giving me a headache." A few seconds of blaring music ticked by until the volume became a more bearable level, allowing her to speak without shouting. "Thank you."

The shifter grunted. "I'll keep the music down as long as you remain silent. If you start talking, I'll turn it up again."

Rather than point out the loud music had to hurt his delicate shifter hearing, Claire merely nodded. Battling Aidan Scott over something as silly as the music wasn't worth the chance of him turning around and dropping her back at her car.

Tapping her fingers against her thigh, every cell in her body urged her to talk with him and find out information. But through sheer force of will, Claire kept her mouth shut.

Even though she could recite her presentation notes and demands in her sleep, she ran through them again inside her head to ease some of her energy. Aidan's disdain toward her chipped at her confidence. She hoped that Kian and his team would view humans differently. Otherwise, the meeting could fail and her ballot initiative would never pass in November.

Rather than think of how the last five years of her life working toward shifter marriage equality could all be for nothing, Claire practiced facts and figures. She'd find out how the cougar-shifters viewed her soon enough.

~~~

Aidan spent the next twenty minutes alternating between tapping his fingers against the steering wheel and gripping it tightly enough to turn his knuckles white. Claire was keeping her end of the bargain and hadn't said a word. Yet despite her silence, he couldn't think of anything but the human female at his side.

Her delicate scent of lavender and woman filled the inside of the car, which only made his inner cougar wake up and take notice. All his cat wanted to do was pull over, cup the human's face, and find out what she tasted like with a kiss. Even Aidan's cock was semi-hard, and only through his learned self-control as a DarkStalker soldier did he keep it from going rock hard.

More than being tortured with her scent, the human half of him tried to figure out why Claire affected him. He'd ridden with countless females from his clan in this very same car and had never had the urge to pull one into his lap and breathe in the scent from where her neck met her shoulder.

He hadn't felt this way in more than ten years. The last time a female's scent had triggered both man and cat, it had been the first time he'd met his dead mate, Emily.

No. Aidan refused to equate the two. While shifters could have several mates in a lifetime, his inner cougar wasn't cruel enough to make him want a human female. Humans were the ones who had stolen his mate from him in the first place.

As Aidan made the last turn and pulled into the back entrance to DarkStalker, he pushed all thoughts of mates, both former and future, out of his mind. Once he handed Claire over to Kian, he'd never see the female again. It would be easy enough to forget her.

Turning off the car, he ordered, "Stay inside and don't take off the mask," and exited before the human could speak. To clear his head, Aidan took in a deep inhalation of fresh air filled with scents of the surrounding forests and lake. He was home.

With his head cleared, he moved to the passenger side of the car and opened the door. While the top half of the female's face was covered, he could see the grim line of her mouth, her plump lips tempting both man and cat to taste them.

Pushing aside his cougar's desires, Aidan kept his tone brisk. "In case you haven't figured it out, we're here."

Claire turned her head up in his general direction. "Can I take off my mask now?"

"No."

She sighed. "Then how am I supposed to walk? And please don't tell me you're going to carry me because that's not going to happen, buddy."

When she slapped a hand over her mouth, Aidan struggled to keep his face neutral. Thankfully, more than twenty years of training won out. "I'll guide you through the passageway."

She removed her hand and revealed her pink, enticing lips again before raising a hand. "Thank you. I greatly appreciate your help."

He resisted a growl. Her sudden politeness and distance grated against his inner cat.

Taking her hand, he pulled her up to her feet so fast she fell into him. As her soft breasts and belly pressed against his chest, a surge of heat shot straight to his cock. Images of Claire Davis naked and him caressing her skin as he sucked her hard nipple filled his mind.

The human's heart rate kicked up and her voice was breathy when she finally spoke up. "Are we going to stand her all day or are we going?"

Her sass snapped Aidan out of his fantasy of taking long licks between Claire's thighs. Afraid the human felt his hard cock pressing against his jeans, he stepped back and turned her until she stood next to his side. "Get ready to walk."

With her hand on his arm and his other hand on her lower back, he pressed her forward. Her standing next to him was too close, and no matter what image he tried to recall to soften his cock, nothing worked. It seemed his cat wanted Claire Davis.

Not that he expected to find an answer in the five minutes it would take to bring Claire to his leader, Aidan ran through all the ways he could purge the human female from his system, because there was no way in hell he was going to pursue her, let alone fuck her. For once, his inner cat wasn't going to get what he wanted.

CHAPTER THREE

Claire knew she should be rehearsing the data one last time before meeting with DarkStalker's leader, but all she could think about was the shifter at her side. In particular, her skin was still hot from falling against his chest. She only hoped that Aidan, let alone other shifters, couldn't scent the betrayal of her body to his touch. Being aroused when she met Kian Murray wasn't exactly what she'd planned.

Yet she couldn't ignore the wetness between her thighs or Aidan's strong hands as he guided her down a series of passageways. For such a tall, muscled man, his touch was delicate against her back.

Of course, it could be because he didn't want to touch her, but she ignored that possibility. She would enjoy a few moments of a shifter's strong touch because that would be all she would ever have.

Sure, she'd done what most teenage girls did and dreamed of having her own shifter to marry. By the time Claire was twenty years old, she'd given up that fantasy. Not only was the marriage between shifters and humans illegal, she'd dedicated herself to her studies, which had brought Claire to her present position as head of the Shifter Equality Alliance. She couldn't afford to be connected to any shifter, not even a one-night stand. The reason so many politicians and other humans listened to her was because the fight wasn't personal.

Well, to the public it seemed impersonal and Claire planned to keep it that way.

Aidan moved his hand from her lower back to her side and squeezed, bringing her back to the present. *Okay, Claire. Stop with the teenage shifter fantasies. No sex with shifters until after the vote in November; that's the rule.* She needed to reinforce boundaries with Aidan.

She turned her head toward Aidan. "Squeeze me again, and I don't care if I'm blindfolded, I will find a way to trip you and call out for help. I'm sure someone will hear me since my voice would echo down the hall."

He grunted. "Stop talking so loudly."

Claire listened for a few seconds and heard a snort a few feet behind them. "Who's there?"

A woman's voice spoke up from behind them. "It's about time someone wasn't drooling over you as they stared into your eyes." The voice became high-pitched. "Oh, Aidan. I want to feel that hard body over me. For someone as handsome as you, I'll even let you take me from behind, no strings attached."

Aidan tightened his grip on her side. His voice was gruff. "Shut up, Dani. If you're as all-seeing as you claim, then you know who this is. You're giving a bad impression of the clan."

The woman who must be Dani replied, "Oh, I know who she is, but I'm curious as to why she's snuggled into your side."

Claire was tired of being talked about. "I'm right here and I don't appreciate what you're implying, especially since I can't see you."

The woman sounded amused. "So, you do have a backbone. Good, I was starting to wonder if my information on you was correct or not."

If Claire's eyes were open, she'd blink. "What information?"

"Nothing of importance to you. Now, Aidan, hurry up. You're late and Kian's waiting."

She half expected Aidan to place the blame on Claire's shoulder. Then he spoke. "I would've been there already if you hadn't butted your nose into my business. We'll talk later."

Aidan pressed against her back, and as they walked, she heard, "Oh, I bet we will. You're not going to like your new assignment."

More confused than ever, Claire moved her head up in what she thought was Aidan's face. "What is she talking about?"

The shifter grunted. "I have no fucking idea."

~ ~ ~

Aidan didn't like the tone of Dani's voice when she mentioned his new assignment. Ever since Sylas Murray had mated the wolves' clan leader, Aidan and Dani had been put in charge of all of DarkStalker's soldiers and security operations. After more than a decade working with Danika Fisher, Aidan knew that particular tone meant nothing but trouble and irritation for him.

Forget it. To be honest, Dani had every right to tease him. As soon as one of DarkStalker's males had walked by, the other male's gaze had drifted to Claire's breasts. The urge to punch him had been overwhelming. At least, until he'd placed his hand on Claire's hip.

His hand remained on her hip. The combined warmth and softness only made his cock harder.

Then the door to the conference room came into sight and Aidan struggled to get his dick under control. In the next few minutes, Claire would no longer be his responsibility. Lusting over her curves was pointless.

Just outside the door, he brought them both to a halt. Claire turned her face toward him and he zeroed in on her lips. If he could only take one kiss, then he could prove to his cougar the human wasn't for them.

As she let out a breath, his head moved forward of its own accord. Her voice was breathy. "Aidan?"

He was half an inch from tasting her sweet lips when the door to the conference room opened and Aidan moved away from Claire's face. Thanks to his shifter reflexes, he was merely standing next to Claire when Kian Murray peeked his head out. "I was wondering where you were. Come, bring her inside."

Claire whispered, "Can I take the mask off now?"

"No."

Claire readjusted her grip on her glasses' case. "Then hurry up because I want to be able to see again."

Aware that every shifter in the conference room could hear them, Aidan merely guided the female into the room and shut the door. All eyes looked from him to Claire and back again.

Before he could say a word, Kian's mate, Trinity, chimed in, "You can take the mask off, dear. You probably could've done so once you entered the special cloaked hallway, but judging by Aidan's expression, he wanted to keep his hands on you."

Trinity always poked her nose where it didn't belong. Yet, he wasn't about to argue with her in front of a stranger. In response, he dropped his grip on Claire and took a step away.

From the corner of his eye, he watched the human take off her mask and blink. Then she put on her glasses before glancing around the room. If Claire had been a shifter, she'd be assessing the possible threats in the room. Surely, the soft human female wouldn't be doing the same thing.

Claire straightened her shoulders and looked to Kian. "You must be Kian."

Kian raised an eyebrow. "My picture isn't widely circulated, so I applaud you on your resources."

Even though Aidan knew his clan leader was happily mated, Aidan didn't like the approving look in Kian's eyes. To prevent himself from doing something stupid, like shoving Claire behind his body, Aidan clenched his fingers. As soon as he had an opening, he needed to ask permission to leave.

Unfortunately, Claire responded straight away. "There are a lot of people who would like for me to disappear, so I keep informed. That's why I know about the human living on your land."

If Kian was surprised, he didn't show it. He merely placed his elbows on the table and leaned forward. "We could stand here like two animals circling each other to determine if the other is an enemy, but I'm going to be honest with you, Claire Davis. I'm on your side. I would love nothing more than for my clan member and his mate to come and go as they please without fear of going to jail. However, I won't sacrifice my clan's stability or safety to do so." He motioned toward one of the empty chairs in front of him. "Please, take a seat so we can get started."

As Claire moved to sit down, Aidan jumped on the temporary silence. "Kian, if there's nothing else, I'd like to check on Chloe."

Kian shook his head. "No, you need to take a seat. You're part of this too." Aidan opened his mouth, but Kian beat him to it. "Chloe is with your brother. She'll be waiting for you when we're through here."

If Kian had arranged for Aidan's daughter to be with his brother, then something important was about to take place. Of course, Aidan had no fucking idea what. "Does this have to do with the new assignment Dani mentioned?"

"Yes. Take a seat, Aidan. The clan needs your help with this."

Trinity smiled. "Yes, and more than the clan needing you, I think you'll enjoy it too."

A bad feeling pooled in his stomach. Trinity smiling with mischief in her eyes was never a good sign.

Not wanting to delay the inevitable, Aidan sat down next to Claire and waited to see what was so fucking important.

~ ~ ~

It was taking everything Claire had to keep from gawking at all the gorgeous shifters sitting in the room. She knew most shifters were attractive because of their confidence and primal instincts, but being in a room with a total of four shifters was nearly too much.

Of course, then Aidan mentioned needing to see a woman named Chloe and her desire to gawk vanished. Given the way he'd caressed her side earlier, she'd assumed he was single. Apparently, she'd been a fool.

No more. Despite the heat radiating off Aidan next to her, Claire pushed aside her earlier desires. Leaning her arms on the table, she met Kian's gaze. "As you were honest with me, I'm

31

going to be honest with you, too. The proposed initiative to legalize shifter-human marriages in the state of Washington can't win without open shifter support. At the moment, it's seen as a one-sided crusade."

Kian nodded. "Yes, I've heard the same thing."

Okay, Kian Murray was more on top of her campaign than she'd imagined. She would make sure not to underestimate the man again. "Then let me be frank: I need to know what can be done, within reason, to win your support."

As Kian leaned back in his chair, Claire waited with bated breath. Only when he started talking did she exhale. "You can earn the help of not only DarkStalker, but GreyFire as well on one condition."

She frowned. "GreyFire? You speak for the wolves now?"

A woman with long, black hair and dark, copper-colored skin spoke for the first time. "No, but I do. Kian and I hashed out the requirement earlier."

Taking a better look at the shifter female, her face matched the only mostly out-of-focus photograph she'd been able to find, which was why Claire hadn't recognized her. "You're Kaya Alexie, leader of Clan GreyFire."

Kaya nodded. "That would be me. Fulfill Kian's request, and you'll have two clans helping you instead of one."

Her heart pounding in her chest, Claire tried to remain calm. Two clans helping her campaign would almost certainly win her the vote in November. Her only concern was what it would cost her.

She looked to Kian. "Then what is it I have to do?"

Kian didn't hesitate. "You'll live with DarkStalker for one month and help teach our clan more about humans."

Claire shook her head. "I don't understand. You already have a human living here. Why do you need me to do this?"

Kaya spoke up. "Because Lauren's a dentist. You, on the other hand, have firsthand knowledge of political processes and how to gauge public opinions. Marriage equality is just the first step. We no longer want to be second-class citizens, and to do that, we need more knowledge if we're to wage a fair battle. You can help us learn how to liaise with humans to change the status quo."

Given the shittiness of the law, Claire wasn't surprised at the shifters wanting to change them.

Still, a million thoughts raced through Claire's head. While she would love nothing more than the chance to live with a clan of shifters for a short period to understand them better, there were a few problems. "If I were to do that, then my name would be tainted and my neutrality compromised. Not only that, I won't be able to work on my campaign. There are only six months before the shifter-human marriage vote takes place. I don't have a month to spare."

Kian leaned back in his chair. "I understand your concerns, but I've considered all of that. You often work out of town, right?" She nodded slowly. "Then you can remain involved with your people via phones and video conferences. I have people who can protect your location with changing IP addresses and much more. No one, apart from high-level FBI investigators, will know you're on my land. Believe me, our clan has become rather good at living under the radar. We had to, or we wouldn't have survived this long."

Claire wished it were that simple. "Let's say you can do everything you mentioned, that still won't allow me to visit with politicians and my other allies for face-to-face meetings. Those have been crucial in garnering support and finances."

Kian shrugged. "Your second-in-command, Ryan Nguyen, can handle those. I know you often split the meetings between you two anyway and you can come up with an excuse, such as having the flu, for why you have to hand off the meetings to him."

She scrutinized Kian's face for a second. "How do you know so much about me?"

Kaya jumped in. "Let's just say we have our contacts."

Claire looked between the clan leaders. "I still don't understand why you picked me for this. There are probably other savvy organizers fighting for shifter equality with much more free time on their hands than me."

One corner of Kian's mouth ticked up. "Because, Claire, you're hardworking and have dedicated a good portion of your life toward shifter equality to help your family and family means everything to a shifter. Don't you think your aunt deserves to come home?"

Claire blinked. "What did you say?"

Kian waved a hand in dismissal. "Don't waste time denying it. I know your aunt eloped with a shifter eleven years ago and is in hiding. That's right around the time when you changed your focus and energy from human rights to shifter rights."

Stomach churning, Claire struggled to keep her wits. If Kian knew about her Aunt Gwen and her shifter partner, then who else knew? Had Gwen's disappearance been more permanent than Claire had realized? Had she been caught?

No. She'd heard from her aunt six months ago. They exchanged anonymous letters once a year, whenever her aunt had found a new place to hide. If something had happened to her,

Gwen's man or his family would've let Claire know somehow since they all moved around together as a pack.

She looked at Kian in a new light. He could probably outdo the FBI when it came to intelligence gathering, if he put his mind to it. "Of course I want her to come home, but if you're going to use my aunt's relationship to force my hand, then you aren't the leader I thought you were."

The female shifter sitting next to Kian gave him a shove. "Stop being so obtuse and threatening; you're pissing off the poor human." The woman looked to her. "I'm Trinity, Kian's mate. Since my mate is botching this up, let me try. We're not trying to force your hand in any way, my dear. We would never endanger your aunt's safety. However, I think we could both benefit from your staying here. If we can get the ShadowClaw bears to join in on this, then you could make a huge difference; not just in shifter-human marriages, but for all of the Cascade shifter clans. Won't you help us? It's only for a month and I will personally make sure you're treated like a queen." Trinity waved a hand toward Aidan. "Aidan will help with that."

The shifter at Claire's side had been silent, but his deep voice filled the small room. "And what, exactly, are you going to make me do?"

Trinity looked back to Claire. "I need Claire's answer first." The shifter female smiled. "Will you help us, dear? What you do with the Cascade shifter clans could set a trend for the whole country."

She looked at Kian, Trinity, Kaya, and finally, Aidan. Given what they already knew about her, protesting about a boyfriend or family missing her would be pointless. Her social life was non-existent outside of work, and her only family was her exiled aunt.

Most of her friends were part of the Shifter Equality Alliance, which meant she could keep in touch via video conferences.

Not to mention she liked the idea of helping to set a trend for shifter rights. She'd only spent the last decade trying to figure out how to make that happen.

There were only two things holding her back. "If I said yes, I couldn't tell anyone, could I? Not even my second-in-command?"

Kaya shook her head. "No. Even those with good intentions can screw things up with a slip of the tongue. Your time here would be against the law. We can protect you while you're on our land since the authorities are afraid to come here after the near-epidemic last year, but our reach only goes so far. We can't risk critical details getting out that could compromise the clan's safety."

Claire remembered hearing about the deadly shifter virus outbreak via her contacts. But she'd confirmed it was safe before coming here. "Okay, but I have one last concern. How can I ensure that your clan will keep my presence a secret, let alone not take out their hatred on me?"

Kian's eyes turned hard. "Believe me, there are no traitors in my clan. We've kept Lauren Spencer-Fisher's presence a secret for nearly four months. Yours will be a walk in the park in comparison since you'll only be staying a month. As for the hatred, my security team will be monitoring the situation closely and will squash any threats they find."

Rubbing her hands against her jeans under the table, Claire tried to make a decision. Daydreaming about living with shifters was one thing, but living with them twenty-four-seven was quite another. She would be the outsider.

Not to mention Aidan Scott would have a hand in something related to her stay. She was pretty sure he'd been close to kissing her earlier when his breath had tickled against her lips. Yet he had a Chloe waiting for him. She didn't want to fight off unwanted attention her entire stay here.

However, if he became a serious problem, she had a feeling Kian might compromise. Or, at least, he would with Trinity's influence. After all, the female shifter had promised to have Claire treated like a queen.

Kian raised his brows. "So, what do you say? Will you accept my offer?"

She gave a sweeping look before meeting Kian's green eyes again. "Will I be treated like a prisoner or will I have free rein?"

Kian and Trinity shared a glance before Kian replied, "For the first week, Aidan will accompany you everywhere. If he reports back that you aren't a threat, you will be allowed free rein in most of the clan spaces. However, a few will remain off limits as they are off limits to any visitors."

Aidan shifted in his seat next to her, but Claire resisted looking at him. "Well, if you can provide me with clothes and retrieve my car, which has my laptop and other important documents, then yes, I accept your offer. However, I want your word that you'll work with me to help ensure the vote passes."

Kian nodded. "Done. I'll give you the rest of the day to settle in and we can talk further over breakfast tomorrow." He then looked to Aidan. "As for the answer to your question, you're going to be Claire's personal guard while she lives here, Aidan."

CHAPTER FOUR

Aidan pushed aside his cougar's happiness at knowing Claire would be staying with them. A whole month in the human's presence would be the ultimate test of his self-control, especially since he wouldn't ruin his leader's plan by letting his dick rule his brain. He needed to convince his leader to pick someone else. "Kian, there are several other candidates who could do the job. Dani needs my help maintaining the clan's security and safety."

Kian merely raised an eyebrow. "We can talk more about that in private. For now, you have your assignment, Aidan. It's an important one, too. Remember that."

Aidan wanted nothing more than to ask why he hadn't been kept in the loop. But from the corner of his eye he could see Claire watching him and he wouldn't castigate his clan leader in front of the human.

Instead, he merely nodded. "Fine. But I need to know where to take her and then I want a private meeting."

Kian stood up and everyone else followed suit. "Of course. Take Claire to the empty set of apartments across from yours."

He frowned. "What? That's in the soldiers' wing."

"I know. It's one of the safest places inside the clan. Besides, Lauren lives near there, too. Claire could use a friend."

Claire spoke up from beside him. "I don't mean to be disrespectful, but I am standing right here."

Aidan's cougar urged him to look at the human female. Since it would be pointless to resist, he did and all he could think about was how her curvy body would be living mere feet away from his. Even now, he imagined taking off her glasses and fisting a hand in her long, light brown hair.

Fucking cougar, stop it. She is our assignment, nothing more.

His cat grumbled, but reluctantly retreated. At least, for now. Aidan looked back to Kian. "Who will watch her while I'm away?"

"Dani."

He wanted to say that was a bad idea, but thought better of it. Kian could only be swayed with reason, and for the moment, Aidan was feeling anything but reasonable, let alone logical. He needed time to think of a way out of this assignment.

Once Aidan nodded, Kian, Kaya, and Trinity walked around the table to stand in front of Claire. The human was nearly a foot shorter than the shifters. It would be easy for him to shield her body from Kian's view.

At that thought, he clenched a jaw and waited. He didn't trust himself to say anything until asked.

Kian put out a hand. "While I had to force your hand a bit to agree to this, I think we'll both benefit from the situation."

Claire shook Kian's hand and Aidan clenched his jaw harder. "It had better, because if you try to screw me over, Kian Murray, I will find a way to use it against you. I have my own set of connections."

Kaya laughed. "Good, a woman with bite. Don't be easy on him. I'm mated to his brother, so I have lots of experience at keeping Murray shifter males in line."

Trinity leaned against Kian and added, "Oh, I'll keep Kian in line. I'm the one who will be able to help you the most, Claire. I can be quite persuasive."

As Kian merely shook his head, memories of Aidan's own dead mate filled his mind. He and Emily had once been like Kian and Trinity. Yet Emily had been stolen from him after only a few years of being mated. He was long past asking why, but it didn't mean it was any less painful to watch two mates in love tease each other. Or, to touch each other on a whim.

He'd taken all of that for granted and regretted it to this day.

Claire dropped Kian's hand. "When can I contact my second-in-command?"

Kian replied, "In the next day or two. We'll set up secure access to the internet tomorrow. However, when you do contact him, Aidan will be in the background for the first few times, just to make sure nothing slips."

Irritation flashed in Claire's eyes and Aidan moved to her side. Placing a hand on her back, some of his cougar's tension eased. "Unless there's anything else, I'll take her to her apartments and get her settled. Have Dani stop by in about twenty minutes."

Since it was Aidan and Dani's job to protect the clan, Aidan was allowed to order Kian in matters of clan security. His clan leader nodded. "Sounds good. Now, take Claire to her quarters."

Before Claire could do much more than open her mouth, Aidan pushed against her back. With a glare in his direction, she moved. He wasn't quick enough, however, because as he shut the door behind them, he could hear Trinity's voice. "Don't have too much fun, you two. Remember, Dani will drop by soon."

Claire whispered, "What the hell is she talking about?"

Rather than answer, Aidan slammed the door and got them moving again.

~~~

As Aidan made them half-jog down the hallway, Claire dug in her heels. With a growl, the shifter looked down at her. "What?"

She poked him in the chest. "Don't growl at me. I understand that babysitting me is the last thing you want to be doing, but it wasn't my call. Don't take it out on me."

"I'm not, but we have twenty minutes to get you settled in. I can answer your questions inside your quarters. Ears are everywhere. Remember that."

He pressed gently against her back. What had once been a strong, firm touch only reminded Claire of how Aidan had someone else. Maybe if they hurried, she could spend most of the remaining twenty minutes freshening up. Then she could grill the shifter named Dani about Aidan. Claire liked to know who she was working with.

With a new goal in mind, she moved her feet again and ignored Aidan to study her surroundings.

The hallway was nothing more than a tunnel carved into the rock of the mountain. There were lights evenly spaced apart, as well as occasional vents, in the ceiling. Despite the fact they'd been walking for a few minutes, there hadn't been any other doors or corridors running off the current one.

While she had intended to wait for questions, she couldn't help but ask, "Why is this hallway nothing but a hallway? Isn't Clan DarkStalker supposed to live in a series of caverns and rooms inside one of the Cascade Mountains?"

He grunted. "I thought we agreed no questions."

She lowered her voice for a dramatic whisper. "I somehow doubt asking about a hallway is a matter of clan secrecy. Unless this leads to a high security prison, where you stash all of your human captives. Maybe that's where all the missing hikers are staying."

Aidan sighed and glanced down at her. "No, we don't imprison hikers. It's much more fun to scare them away with a cougar howl."

"Then explain about the hallway and why you made me wear a mask before if this is all there was to see."

He stared at her a second before replying, "This is the safe hallway we use for visitors. It protects said visitors from accessing our most vulnerable. Until you agreed to Kian's plan, we didn't want you to see anything of our land, apart from the conference room."

"So I was considered a threat?"

"Every stranger is considered a threat."

Considering the long, bloody history between not only shifters and humans, but also among shifter clans, she couldn't blame the precaution. "I hope I'm not constantly going to be viewed as a threat for the entire month I'm here. Otherwise, no one will listen to anything I say. They'll think I'm lying."

"Most of the clan knows you by name, if not face. You're well-known among the shifter clans of Washington State for your work with the Shifter Equality Alliance."

She blinked. "I am?"

"Yes." He waved up ahead. "We're about to turn into the soldiers' living area, so I need you to remain silent until we enter your apartment."

Claire was used to being in charge, but she had learned a long time ago to pick her battles. This one wasn't worth it.

As they approached a door, Aidan typed in a code into a security panel. The lock clicked, and he guided her through.

The instant they turned a corner, the atmosphere changed. Warm lights lined the walls, in between doors painted in different colors. A few even had decorations or signs on them. One door they passed had a sign which said, "Beware: Guard Cat Inside." Claire smiled. That particular soldier or family clearly had a sense of humor.

One of the doors opened, revealing a dark-skinned woman wearing a loose sweater top and jeans. Claire had seen her picture before. It was Lauren Spencer, the human who had disappeared four months ago to live with the shifters.

When Lauren met her eyes, her smile was warm. "Is this her?"

Aidan stopped in front of the woman and Claire followed suit. "Yes, this is Claire. However, we don't have time to talk. You can visit her later."

Lauren shook her head. "Oh, Aidan, you don't have to be so serious." Lauren's brown eyes met hers. "I'm Lauren. Kian probably told you about me, and if you ever need another human to talk with, I live here with my mate."

Claire couldn't help but smile back at Lauren. "You're mated to a soldier?"

Lauren grinned. "No, although he likes to think he is one. He's an engineer. We live here for protection, the same as you."

Before Aidan could say anything, Claire asked, "Did it take long for you to adjust to living inside a mountain?"

Lauren shrugged. "I venture outside often with my mate, as his cat goes stir-crazy otherwise." Lauren leaned toward Claire. "If you want my advice, don't show fear and the cougars will accept you a lot quicker. It worked for me."

Claire was about to say she should have no trouble doing that when Aidan pressed against her back and grunted. "Sorry, Lauren. We really need to go."

Lauren tilted her head. "Before you leave, just one more question: where is Claire staying?"

"In the empty rooms across from mine."

Lauren studied Aidan a second. "Don't sound so happy about it, okay?"

To keep from laughing at Lauren's sarcasm, Claire bit her lip a second. "It's nice to meet you, but if we don't leave soon, Aidan will probably start snarling. Besides, all I want to do after trekking through the snow is to take a hot shower. I hope to see you around."

Lauren nodded. "Of course. See you later."

Aidan turned Claire down another hallway and Claire decided she would seek out Lauren later. If the rumors were true, Lauren's mate had survived a kidnapping by Human Purity. The anti-shifter group was one of Claire's enemies and she could use more information on them to help figure out strategies.

However, soon Aidan stopped them in front of a dark blue door and she looked up at him. His voice was gruffer than she'd ever heard before. "We're here."

~~~

All Aidan could think about was Claire's naked body being sprayed with hot water. In his mind, as the water droplets cascaded down her breasts, her waist, and eventually between her thighs, he wanted to lick her dry.

RESISTING THE COUGAR

Fucking cougar. Stop with the sex fantasies.

His inner cat merely swished a tail. The goddamn animal was enjoying Aidan's discomfort.

Arriving at Claire's new quarters, he struggled to get his brain and cock under control. Even to his own ears, his voice was forced. "We're here."

After opening the door, he motioned Claire inside. Giving him a strange look, she thankfully entered without another word. Of course, as she walked in front of him, he couldn't resist looking at her large, shapely ass.

Claire's voice broke through his admiration and he quickly looked up before she turned around. "It's not what I expected."

He shut the door and crossed his arms over his chest. "Don't tell me, you expected us to have straw beds and holes in the ground for toilets?"

She glared. "No, of course not. But all of the furnishings are made from wood, and not the cheap imitation stuff you get at most stores."

Despite himself, the corner of Aidan's mouth ticked up. "We prefer everything real over fake. Our inner animals aren't fond of processed materials."

"By that argument, you wouldn't touch a car with a ten-foot pole."

He shrugged. "We had to learn to adapt or we would've died out a long time ago. You've worked with shifters long enough to know how stubborn we are. Scold your inner cougar enough, and they'll grudgingly accept change."

"That's good to know. Maybe I can find a way to use that stubbornness to my advantage."

Oh no. "Don't get any ideas, human. If you are planning to trick Kian, he'll see through it in a matter of seconds."

Amusement twinkled in her eyes. "I never said I would use it on Kian."

"Or on me. It won't work."

Claire grinned and Aidan felt like he'd been punched in the gut. Her smile lit up the whole room.

His gaze focused yet again on her lips, the sight of them heating his blood. His cat growled, wanting to taste her.

It took everything he had to push aside his inner cougar and look back to Claire's eyes. The grin was gone, replaced with something hotter. If he were delusional, he might think she wanted to kiss him too.

Clearing her throat, Claire broke the tension. "So, are you going to give me a tour?"

As he guided her around the kitchen, living area, and bathroom, he counted down from one hundred inside his head to cool his blood. He'd gotten his dick under control by the time they reached the bedroom. But as Claire sat down on the queen-sized bed and rubbed her hand on the smooth, dark blue comforter, his cat urged him to cover her with his body and steal a kiss.

He took a step toward the bed, and then another. Claire looked up at him, her eyes stubborn and he stopped. She asked, "Who's Chloe?"

He blinked. "Why are you asking me that?"

She frowned. "I need to know who I'm working with. You keep giving me sex eyes and I want to know if you're the kind of man to sleep with anyone without thought or not."

With a growl, he took a step toward her, using his height to try to intimidate her. Too bad the damn woman didn't so much as bat an eyelash at him. His heart pumped harder as anger gathered in his gut. Narrowing his eyes, he didn't keep the menace out of his tone. "I would never cheat on a female. The fact you think I would is highly insulting. You know nothing about me, Claire Davis, so don't judge me. Maybe you aren't the female I thought you were."

~~~

Claire stood up, not caring that she was only a few inches from Aidan's broad chest. "I was going to wait until Dani came to ask her, but I'd rather hear it from you. Tell me who Chloe is and set me straight on what type of man you are, Aidan Scott. If you refuse, I'll ask for another babysitter."

"You won't ask for anyone else."

The heat of his gaze as well as his body made her heart rate kick up. Aidan was pure shifter male, every inch of his muscles making her weak in the knees. He was the type of tall, dark stranger she'd never had a chance with. Why she was standing here, asking him about Chloe, she didn't know. If anything, her behavior could make her stay with DarkStalker even more difficult.

But as his gaze bore into hers, she licked her lips. His eyes followed the action, and wetness rushed between her legs. She'd never wanted to kiss a man so much in her life as she did in that moment. She was drawn to his scent, his touch, and even the spattering of gray hair at his temples.

For the first time, Claire started to understand what some of her friends had said about having no control over attraction.

She finally forced herself to reply. "You aren't the boss of me, Aidan, so stop ordering me around. I'm not one of your soldiers."

Aidan took the remaining step between them. If Claire so much as took a deep breath, her hard nipples would brush against his chest. On instinct, her nipples tightened further, aching to feel Aidan's hard chest.

What the hell is happening to me?

Aidan's hot breath tickled her forehead. "No, you're not, which is why you're dangerous."

Eyes glowing the same amber as she'd seen earlier in his cougar-form, her heart rate beat even faster. Seeing his animal side in his gaze made her pussy ache. She wondered what all of that raw power and animal magnetism would be like when they were both naked.

No, you can't. Remembering how getting involved with a shifter sexually could threaten her campaign, Claire tried to take a step back. Aidan's hands went to her waist, trapping her where she stood. She whispered, "I don't know you. I just can't."

An emotion she couldn't define flashed in his eyes before his deep voice caressed her ears. "Chloe is my daughter. I don't have a mate."

"Daughter?"

"Yes." He moved a hand to trace her cheek and then her lower lip. Claire melted a little at his touch. Yet somehow she remained standing as he continued, "Yes, you can, Claire Davis. I need to know."

She swallowed. "Know what?"

Lowering his head until he was a hair's breadth from her lips, he whispered, "I need to know how you taste or I won't be able to function properly."

Claire's mouth went dry. No man had ever needed to kiss her so badly in her life. She looked to Aidan's firm lips, so masculine yet probably soft to the touch. Surely one kiss wouldn't ruin her reputation. No one was here but her and Aidan, and she had a feeling that Aidan wouldn't tell anyone. After all, it could damage his clan and if he really was as important of a protector as she was guessing he was, he would cut off his own leg before harming anyone inside DarkStalker.

Looking back into his eyes, she raised her head. She opened her mouth to tell him to kiss her when there was a knock on the door.

Aidan jumped back like he'd been burned. As he looked at her, he ran a hand through his dark hair. The hungry expression had been replaced with a neutral one she couldn't read. Claire didn't like his remoteness one bit.

The cougar-shifter cleared his throat. "That will be Dani. I'll talk to her while you shower. She'll be in the living area when you're done."

Before she could say anything, Aidan was out the door, leaving her alone in the bedroom. Any heat or desire she'd felt was gone, as if someone had thrown a bucket of ice water over her head.

Rather than dwell on the rejection, she went into the bathroom and locked the door. As she undressed and turned on the simple showerhead inside the standing shower stall, Claire realized how Dani's knock had saved her from doing something extremely stupid. No matter how attracted she was to Aidan Scott, she couldn't kiss him.

Stepping under the hot spray of water, Claire closed her eyes. Whatever had just happened was a onetime thing. Next time, she would be able to resist the cougar. The happiness of her aunt, and every other human who fell in love with a shifter, depended on Claire succeeding. Kissing a shifter, any shifter, would have to wait six months.

By then, Aidan Scott wouldn't be anything more than a distant memory.

Chapter Five

Aidan's cougar snarled and tried to break free as soon as he walked out of the bedroom. His cat wanted the human. Dani could wait until they were done.

Rather than argue, he clenched his fingers and stretched them out. Repeating the process, he muscled to take full control of his mind. The last thing he needed was for Dani to spot his glowing cougar eyes and guess what he'd been about to do.

And Aidan was pretty sure the human had been about to ask him to kiss her.

With some distance, he grew angry with himself. Why he'd told Claire that Chloe was his daughter, he didn't know. His life would be a whole lot easier if he'd not answered and let her assume the worst of him.

Besides that, giving in to the pull of the human's magnetism brought on a sense of guilt. The crazy drive to kiss the living shit out of someone had only belonged to Emily. If he'd gone through with it, it would've felt like betrayal.

Memories of his mate's brown eyes and dark, curly hair helped to calm down his cougar. If given the chance, both man and cat would do anything to caress Emily's light brown skin again. For Chloe's sake, he needed to keep her memory alive.

Arriving at the door, Aidan took one last deep breath. With any luck, Dani wouldn't guess anything was out of the ordinary.

He opened the door and stood to the side. As soon as Dani entered, Aidan instructed, "Claire's taking a shower. I told her you would wait out here. I don't know how long I'll be since I hope to check on Chloe, but if it's too long, I'll call you."

Dani raised an eyebrow. "I'm not one of your soldiers to boss around, Aidan. You only do that when you're trying to hide something from me."

"I'm not going to defend myself. If anyone has been hiding something, it's you, Danika. Why didn't you tell me about my assignment as Claire's bodyguard?"

Dani shrugged. "I didn't know myself until you had left. Kian, Kaya, and Trinity picked you."

"I still don't understand why me. Lauren's parents are due for another visit soon. I'd much rather plan how to sneak them onto our land without being noticed."

Dani plopped down on the couch. "In my personal view, I think they gave you this assignment because you work too hard. Take it easy for a while, Aidan. Five years is a long time."

He growled. "We agreed for you not to meddle in my personal life."

"It's my concern when your built-up sexual energy starts to interfere with your work. Frankly, I don't care if you fuck the human or another female. Just do it and do it soon. Then you'll be a lot less growly."

"Stay out of my business, Dani."

Dani raised her hands. "Judging by the way the human's scent covers you, you're halfway there already."

"I have a meeting with Kian. While I'm gone, don't give any ideas to the human. I have no plans to touch her."

Amusement flashed in Dani's eyes. "We'll see. I haven't decided if I like her or not. If I do end up liking her, well, I won't make any promises."

"Whatever, I don't have time for this. Just protect her."

Before Dani could reply, Aidan exited Claire's apartments and went into his own. He wasn't about to meet Kian Murray covered in Claire's scent. He already had Dani on his case; he didn't need anyone else, especially since he planned to keep his distance. He'd slipped up earlier, but he wouldn't do it again. She was his assignment, nothing more.

~ ~ ~

Since Claire didn't have any other clothes, after her shower, she merely put back on her jeans and thermal t-shirt. Her hair would have to air dry. Of course, it wasn't like she was trying to impress anyone. If anything, she needed to dissuade Aidan. Maybe muddy clothes and frizzy hair would do the trick.

Adjusting her glasses on her nose, Claire took a deep breath and exited the bathroom. A woman with red hair in a French braid lounged on her couch, looking at her cell phone. The female must be Dani, the shifter woman she'd heard earlier in the corridor, when Claire had been blindfolded. "Hello."

Dani glanced over, her eyes a deep blue. "I heard you exit the bathroom, but wanted to give you the chance to work up your nerve."

"Right, because you're such a scary shifter."

Dani gave a thumbs up. "Glad you realize that already."

Claire crossed her arms over her chest. Unlike when she was with Aidan, she didn't have the urge to tease back. It was more awkward with Dani.

As the silence stretched, the shifter's blue-eyed gaze studied her like a test subject, not wanting to miss a detail. Instead of shuffling her feet, Claire straightened her shoulders and forced herself to ask, "Aidan didn't mention anything about my belongings, let alone about new clothes. I can't wear these every day for a month. Do you know when they'll come?"

Dani smiled and sat up. "Straight to the point. I like that." Standing up, Dani towered nearly a foot over Claire's head. "I was just checking on the status of your car. We should have it here in a few hours. The fog is making things difficult."

Play it cool, not like you got lost. "And clothes?"

"You're shorter and rounder than most of the shifters, but I might be able to scrounge something up. Actually, wait right here a second."

Dani exited the door.

Claire blinked. *What the hell just happened?*

Before she could think much more about it, Dani returned with a pile of clothes in her arms. After dumping them on the couch, she rifled through them and held up a large shirt, sweatshirt, and sweatpants, all black. "Go put these on."

"Right now?"

Dani shoved them into her arms and turned her toward the bathroom. "I know humans are shy or I'd strip you myself. Just do it."

Claire frowned and looked over her shoulder. "Do all shifters like to order people around?"

Grinning, Dani gave her a shove. "Only the best ones do." She winked. "Hurry, I want you changed before Aidan comes back."

"Um, why?"

"Just do it and I'll answer any questions you might have with no bullshitting around. Deal?"

If it took her putting on some overly large clothes to get answers, Claire would do it. "Fine."

Shutting herself in the bathroom, Claire undressed yet again and put on the new set of clothes. The arms reached past her fingers tips and the sweatpants were miles too long for her legs. The only thing that fit was the waist of the pants since Claire had developed a belly over the last decade.

At least, looking in the mirror, she was about as nondescript as she could get. The billowing, shapeless clothes should dissuade Aidan from kissing her again.

Yet, she swore his scent filled her nose. Raising a sleeve, she took a deep inhalation and was bombarded with a faint male scent of man and forest she was slowly becoming addicted to: Aidan's.

The door opened and Claire frowned at Dani's face. The redhead grabbed her arm and tugged her toward the living room. "I heard you were done. You look perfect."

"Why did you give me Aidan's clothes?"

She shrugged. "I have a key to his place and it was the closest."

Claire could waste what precious minutes she had left asking more about the clothes, but she wanted to know about the clan. Once Dani sat down on the couch, Claire remained standing and crossed her arms. "Who are you, exactly? And don't tell me your name. You seem on equal footing with Aidan, and I'm curious why."

"That's because I am. After Kian's brother mated Kaya and moved to GreyFire's land, Aidan and I were put in charge of security. Of course, I like to think I slightly outrank him."

Claire sat down on the opposite end of the couch. "Then if Aidan's so high up in the ranks, why is he my shadow? I'm in charge of an organization and I would never ask my second-in-command to do a job someone lower on the totem pole could do. It seems like a waste of skills."

Dani assessed her a second before nodding. "I was right about you. You're intelligent. That will help both you and the clan a great deal."

"That still doesn't answer my question about why Aidan is assigned as my shadow."

Shrugging, Dani crossed one leg over the other. "He's devoted the last five years of his life to his work and he's close to snapping. Kian knows it, and decided you might be the answer."

Claire forced her expression to remain neutral. "You'd better explain that better, because as it stands, you make me sound like a mare about to be sent out to stud."

Dani grinned. "I wish I could simply give Aidan a female and calm him down, but it's not that easy. You see, his mate was killed by poachers five years ago."

"What?"

"It's true. Despite the myths, shifters can take a new mate if they wish, once they pass the grieving stage, but Aidan hasn't done so. He's been pretty damn reserved. At least, until he met you."

Claire blinked. "I don't understand. Why are you telling me this?"

"I just figured it was something you should know."

No doubt, Dani had an ulterior motive, but Claire would set her straight. "Listen, if you're trying to clear the path for me to jump into bed with him, it's not going to happen. My work is too important."

Raising an eyebrow, Dani gave her a piercing stare. "I admire your work, but there's no one here who would tell your secrets. I can spot a female who devotes her life to her work at the expense of everything else."

She clenched her jaw. "And how, exactly, can you do that? Some shifter magic I don't know about?"

Dani's smile faded. "No, because I'm the same way. The only difference is I don't have anyone I can turn to because of how far up the hierarchy I am. You, on the other hand, have the chance to help both Aidan and yourself."

Heart beating double-time, Claire struggled to keep her face neutral. "While I'm sorry for your predicament, you won't be able to live your life through mine. I spent the last five years, and more, trying to gain shifter-human equality. I'm not about to allow a hottie to distract me."

"So you do find him attractive."

Claire ignored Dani's statement. "Now, you promised me some answers and I want them. How does everyone know so much about me?"

Dani studied her a second before replying, "I won't give out names, but through our DS Engineering business in Seattle, we have access to a lot of talented humans. Not everyone believes the same as Human Purity or other extremist groups, and they help us out every once in a while."

Human Purity wanted all shifters eradicated, or just about. "If you have all of these talented people, then why didn't you reach out to SEA earlier?"

"The SEA was doing well enough on their own. No matter how much it may grate against my nerves, humans fighting for us does more good than shifters standing up for themselves."

Some of Claire's earlier anger eased. "I know, but you see, that's why my work is so important. I want shifters to be on equal footing and not second-class citizens."

Dani patted the couch beside her. "Sit down, Claire. I'll answer a few more questions, but first, I want to know what kind of shifter your aunt is mated to."

Claire hadn't been able to talk about her aunt in over a decade. The urge to remain quiet was strong, but given how much DarkStalker needed her help, she could probably share general details without getting into trouble. Besides, thinking of her Aunt Gwen, sadness squeezed her heart. Claire missed her.

Sitting down, Claire met Dani's eyes again. "He's a bear, although I've never met him."

"Interesting. The bears around here are mostly lawyers and keep to themselves. I've wondered what they're like."

Claire tucked that piece of information away for later. Maybe she could convince Kian to invite the bears to a meeting. "I don't know, really. I haven't met any of them, either." Claire settled into a more comfortable position. "Now, tell me what you can of the DarkStalker and GreyFire alliance. The more information I have, the more I can implement the alliance into my campaign."

Dani didn't so much as blink at the change of topic. "How much do you know?"

"Not much, just that you worked together to stop an epidemic last year." Dani opened her mouth, but Claire beat her to it. "No, it's not common knowledge. If it were, every anti-shifter group in the world would be developing their own shifter-specific viruses. I, on the other hand, have a number of shifter contacts in the city. I heard it from one of them."

The shifter female looked like she wanted to ask more, but merely nodded. "Rather than press for details, I'll hold up my end of the bargain."

Claire had a feeling Dani would know the names of all Claire's contacts in the city within a matter of days.

The shifter kept her word, though, and went into the details and history of the alliance. As Dani spoke, Claire was able to forget the shifter's earlier comments about Aidan. She may be stuck on DarkStalker's land for the next month, but she had plenty of work to keep her busy. She wouldn't think of Aidan, let alone how he must be hurting from the loss of his mate. From what little she knew about the cougar anyway, he wouldn't want pity or sympathy. Claire had no intention of treating him any differently the next time she saw him.

Well, except for avoiding his touch or kisses. Those she would force herself to do without.

CHAPTER SIX

As Aidan headed back toward Claire's quarters, it took everything he had to keep his expression neutral. The meeting with Kian hadn't gone as he'd liked.

Kian was determined to have Aidan as the human's guard. What bothered Aidan was his clan leader not telling him the specifics of why. His only answer had been, "You need a change."

I don't need a fucking change. He was good at his job. Apparently, he was being punished for working hard.

Questioning his leader's orders was unusual for him, but none of his other assignments had involved being in the same room as Claire Davis. One whiff of her scent would turn his cock hard.

He needed to think of some way to keep distance between them.

Then it hit him. If he brought Chloe with him, then he could focus on his daughter's safety and happiness. Kian hadn't told him he couldn't. Aidan would pounce on the opening.

He made a quick turn and soon arrived at his brother's quarters. After a quick knock, Aidan's younger brother, Jeremy, opened the door with a quizzical look and asked, "Can you tell me why Chloe needed to stay here? I never mind, of course, since my mate loves to look after her. But is there a threat I should know about, brother?"

Aidan shook his head. "No, just a new assignment. I wish I could tell you more, but Kian should make an announcement in the next few days."

Used to Aidan's secrecy, Jeremy nodded. "Can you stay for dinner?"

"No, I need to collect Chloe and get back to work."

Jeremy gave him a curious look, but didn't press the matter.

His daughter rushed out of one of the side rooms. Aidan crouched down and engulfed her in a hug. Chloe's voice was muffled against his chest. "Daddy, you're here."

Breathing in his daughter's light scent of wild flowers, some of Aidan's stress dissipated. "Yes, my little cub, I'm here." He leaned back to smooth Chloe's curly hair from her face. "But I have a special assignment." He lowered his voice to a whisper. "This time, you're going to be my secret partner. Would you like that?"

She squealed before putting on a serious face and whispered, "What's our secret partner assignment?"

"Well, we need to protect a human and make sure she stays out of trouble."

"A human? Like Lauren?"

He nodded. "Yes, baby, like Lauren. Are you up for the challenge?"

Chloe bobbed her head and then wiggled out of his hug. "Let me get my backpack. We can fill it with special soldier tools."

Aidan chuckled as his daughter raced into the next room. Standing up, he looked to Jeremy. "I know you heard me, but don't repeat what I just told Chloe. Your mate is fine, but no one else."

Jeremy nodded. "Of course, but I never thought you would be the one guarding a human."

"It wasn't my decision."

Chloe raced back out, with Aidan's sister-in-law right behind her. Aidan walked over and gave his sister-in-law a hug. "Thanks for helping out with Chloe, Naomi."

Naomi released him. "No problem, Aidan. Whatever this 'secret assignment' is, she's pretty excited about it."

An unanswered question lingered in the air and Aidan decided to answer it. "She won't be in any harm. Believe me, it should be somewhat educational for her."

Naomi studied him a second. "If you say so."

Chloe grabbed his hand and pulled. "Come, Daddy, we should hurry. I want to start our assignment."

Aidan bit back a smile and looked to his brother. "Thanks, Jeremy. I'll stop by in a few days. Hopefully by then, I can fill you in on what's going on."

Chloe tugged his arm again and Aidan gave in to his daughter. She was so determined that she didn't say a word as she practically ran down the hallway. Only when they reached where the corridor split off into different sections did she stop and look at him. "Which way, Daddy?"

"Head toward our home."

She frowned. "Why? I want to get started."

The way Chloe stood there, with a frown and stubborn jaw, reminded Aidan of her mother. At least, he would always have a small part of Emily in their daughter. "Our person to protect is staying across the hallway from us."

Chloe's amber eyes lit up. "Then we can bring her into our apartment sometimes, too. Maybe she wants to play dragons with me."

The image of Claire with her arms out to mimic flying and roaring through the living room made him smile. "You can ask her tomorrow." He covered the few steps between them and leaned down to Chloe's ear. "First, we need to make sure she is safe. Then you can ask her anything you like, okay?"

Chloe nodded enthusiastically. "Good, because I have a lot of questions about humans."

He took his daughter's hand. "Then let's hurry."

As they made their way toward Claire's apartment, Chloe rattled off a list of everything she wanted to ask the human. He smiled. His daughter had always been a gregarious chatterbox. With her in the same room as Claire, Aidan would never have the chance to think of kissing the human, let alone anything else.

Yes, bringing his daughter along was the best idea he'd ever had.

~ ~ ~

Claire had committed to memory the important facts of the DarkStalker and GreyFire alliance. Just as she opened her mouth to grill Dani about DarkStalker's troubles with the anti-shifter groups, there was a knock on the door. Dani stood up. "I'll get it."

When the door opened to reveal Aidan, Claire wanted to tell him to go away. Then a little girl no more than six or seven, with a mass of dark curls, raced inside and stopped in front of her.

Before Claire could do more than blink, the little girl leaned in and whispered, "I'm your second bodyguard. I'm going to make sure there aren't any bad people in your place."

Then the girl raced into Claire's bedroom. A deep, male laugh from the doorway drew her attention. Frowning at Aidan, she demanded, "What the hell just happened?"

Dani shook her head. "That's Chloe, Aidan's daughter." Dani shot an inquiring look at Aidan. "I'm wondering why she's here."

Aidan shrugged. "I can't just turn over my daughter for a month. As long as we're inside DarkStalker's cave system, Chloe is safe enough to stay with me during this assignment." His eyes flashed with amusement as he looked to Claire. "Oh, by the way, I told her she's my partner for this secret assignment. Expect her to play the part."

Claire opened her mouth, but Chloe raced back out and stood in front of her dad. "I didn't find any bad guys. It should be safe here."

Aidan squeezed the little girl's shoulder. "Good." He turned his daughter to face Claire. "Claire, this is my daughter, Chloe. Chloe, Claire Davis is the human we're going to protect for the next month."

Claire wanted to ask Aidan for more specifics, but was mindful of the little girl staring at her with amber eyes. The eyes reminded her of Aidan in his cougar form.

While Claire didn't have any children of her own, she had done her fair share of outreach programs to schools in the area. The first few minutes of meeting a child often dictated how they would treat you forever. If Aidan thought to unsettle her with his daughter, he was in for a surprise.

Standing up, Claire walked over to Chloe and put out a hand. "Nice to meet you, Chloe."

The little girl stared up at her for a second in awe before blinking and taking her hand. After a few enthusiastic pumps, she replied. "What is the weird thing on your face?"

Claire smiled as she touched her glasses. "You mean these?" Chloe nodded. "Well, unlike shifters, some humans can't see very well. If I don't have these special glasses, everything beyond my arm's length is blurry."

"Can I try them?" Chloe asked.

Crouching down, Claire removed her glasses and put them on Chloe's face. "What do you think?"

The little girl blinked a few times. "Everything is fuzzy. How can you see?"

Removing the glasses, Claire put them back on. "That's how I see normally, Chloe, without the glasses. They are very important to me, so one of your missions is to make sure I don't lose them, okay?"

"Okay." Chloe looked up at her dad. "What's next? I want to help."

Claire moved her gaze to Aidan. The smile and warmth in his eyes revealed a loving father beneath his grumpy exterior.

Aidan motioned his head toward the kitchen. "How about you sit at the kitchen table with Dani for a few minutes while I talk with Claire in private?"

Bobbing her head, Chloe rushed to Dani and took her hand. "Come on, Dani. You can give me some tips on how to protect Claire better."

Dani smiled. "I have some really good ideas, Chloe. I'll even tell you some secrets."

Chloe cheered. "Yay, then let's get started." She looked over her shoulder to her father. "You can take a while, Daddy. I want to hear all of Dani's secrets."

Claire only just stopped herself from laughing at Aidan's frown. His deep voice was suspicious. "Just don't give her any dangerous ideas, Danika Fisher."

Dani gave a mock salute and guided Chloe to the table. Claire met Aidan's eyes. "Well? What do you need to tell me?"

He placed a hand on her elbow. "Not here. Come with me."

Opening the door, he brought her out into the hallway. Claire was about to ask again when Aidan unlocked his own door and opened it.

She frowned. "Why are we going in there?"

"Because it's private."

~ ~ ~

After Aidan guided Claire inside his apartment and shut the door, he turned toward her. "Why are you wearing my clothes?"

She shrugged. "Dani gave them to me. As soon as I get my own, you can have them back. I'm sure these aren't the only things you own."

No, they weren't. But Aidan's cougar was purring at the sight of the human wearing their clothes. Not only that, she was currently covered in their scent.

His cougar's possessiveness pulsed throughout his body. The cat didn't care about what the human wanted; he just wanted to kiss Claire.

His eyes must have flashed, because Claire's own widened. "Why do your eyes keep flashing? I know sometimes shifters do that with strong emotions, but I would surely hope you don't hate me that much."

Desire pounded harder. Aidan was close to losing control of his inner cougar. Through gritted teeth, Aidan managed to say, "Yes, my cougar is having some strong emotions, but it sure as hell isn't hate."

Claire took a step back and placed a hand on her chest, drawing his eyes to her plump breasts. "I know what nearly happened before, Aidan, but it's not going to happen again."

With his cat demanding at least Claire's scent, Aidan crossed the distance. Lowering his head to her neck, he took a deep inhalation. The scent of female and lavender calmed his cat a fraction.

Claire's voice was strained. "Aidan? What are you doing?"

His plan to use his daughter as a barrier was failing. Even if they marched back over straight away, Chloe would go to school tomorrow and what then?

He'd be fucked.

Pushing at his control, his cougar urged him to hurry up and kiss the female. That was all he wanted.

Yeah, right. I'm not buying it.

A growl was his answer.

Using his nineteen years' experience as a soldier, he wrestled the cougar back into a mental cage. While the need to kiss the human was still present, it was dull enough to allow him to function.

Moving his head back enough to look down at Claire, he murmured, "What am I doing? The sight of you in my clothes, as well as being covered in my scent, is driving my cougar crazy. When Chloe is around, I hardly notice. But we're going to soon have a problem, Claire."

He could hear Claire's heart beating double-time. "Why?"

Placing a hand on either side of her head, the human's pupils dilated a fraction. The sight only made his cock harder. "Chloe will have to leave for school in the morning."

After a second, Claire answered, "Oh."

"I may have a solution, however."

Fire returned to Claire's gaze. "If you suggest a quickie, I will slap you. I won't be your stud mare."

He blinked. "What the hell are you talking about?"

"Never mind. You need to—"

As soon as his finger made contact with her cheek, Claire stopped talking. Aidan's cat liked how they could make the female speechless.

Aidan stroked Claire's skin, loving how soft it was. She wasn't wearing any make-up, so there was nothing standing between his skin and hers.

More than aware the female might turn her head away from his touch, Aidan moved his thumb to her lower lip. Running it back and forth, the human open her mouth slightly. She whispered, "Aidan...I can't."

Placing his thumb beneath her lip, he murmured, "Can't or won't. One kiss, Claire. That should satisfy my cat long enough to allow me to think of another way to calm him."

"Somehow, I don't believe you."

The corner of his mouth ticked up. "I won't lie to you anymore, nor to myself. I want nothing more than to lick between your thighs and pound into you from behind. But..."

The scent of Claire's arousal instantly filled the room, which made his cat snarl and growl. The female wanted them. They should take her.

The human swallowed. "But, what?"

"I won't hurt my clan's chances of obtaining equal rights. DarkStalker needs your help, Claire, and fucking you and walking away might threaten that."

"Walking away, huh? You sure know how to charm a woman."

"You know what I mean. I have my sentry duties and my daughter. You have your organization and work. Nothing between us would ever work out long-term."

Since when have I thought about keeping her long-term?

His cougar purred at the thought of keeping the human forever.

Claire searched his eyes for a few seconds before finally saying, "You swear this isn't just a ploy to get into my pants? Will it really help calm your cougar long enough to think of another plan?"

Stroking the soft skin under her lip, he shook his head. "I won't get into your pants, Claire. Not unless you ask me to."

Indecision flashed in her eyes. That gave both man and cat small hope she would say yes.

Wait, what? Since when did Aidan the man want to kiss her? His cat hissed. They both wanted her.

Fuck, he was done lying. If he didn't kiss the human soon, not even his daughter in the room would be able to stop him from trying to steal one soon. She had better say yes.

~~~

Claire's heart thundered inside her chest. Aidan's tall, muscled body surrounded hers and she struggled not to lift a hand and pull him closer. She was wet and aching. Never before in her life had she felt as if she would combust if she didn't kiss a man.

Kiss? Hell, she might die if she didn't feel his hard, warm skin under her hands. Then maybe she could explore his skin with her lips before taking his cock into her mouth.

"Claire?"

Aidan's deep voice broke through her sex fantasies. Looking into his eyes, they were glowing again. To an average human, it would be a little terrifying. To Claire, it only emphasized his alpha maleness; Aidan was part animal, and she could never forget that.

Animals acted on instinct, though, so she needed to answer his request, and quickly.

Rationally, she should run across the hall, grab Dani, and have the female shifter take her to Kian. One word and Kian would probably grant her request for a new guard.

Yet her mind screamed at the thought of never having a chance to kiss Aidan.

Dani's words from earlier echoed inside her head. *There's no one here who would tell your secrets.* As long as it was just one kiss when they were alone, no one would find out, let alone ruin her reputation.

For the first time in her life, Claire was going to be bold with a man.

Placing a hand on Aidan's chest, she leaned toward him. His growl shot straight to her pussy. She was fast becoming addicted to his animal side.

Aidan's tone was low and husky when he stated, "I'm going to kiss you, Claire."

Tilting her head up, she whispered, "Then do it."

70

Lowering his head, Aidan's lips touched hers. After a gentle brush, he seamed her lips. On instinct, she opened and he plunged his tongue into her mouth.

As he stroked and sucked, filling her mouth with the delicious taste of Aidan, fire raced through her body, ending between her legs. Before she could do more than stroke back, he grabbed her ass and hauled her up against his body. Her nipples brushed his chest and she moaned.

The sound only made Aidan thread one hand through her hair and take the kiss deeper. All reason gone, she acted on instinct and rubbed against his hard cock poking against her stomach.

Aidan broke the kiss with a hiss. Before she could blink, he took her lower lip between his teeth and nibbled. The slight sting only made her moan louder.

When Aidan moved a hand to her breast and squeezed her sensitive nipple, she sucked in a breath. Why was she wearing such thick clothes? All she could think about was his rough hands on her skin.

Claire was on the verge of asking him to do exactly that when the door pounded behind her and she squealed.

Gathering her against his chest in a protective hold, he snarled at the door, "What?"

"Sorry to cut short your make-out session, but I need to leave," Dani answered in an amused tone.

She waited to see if Aidan would deny Dani's words, but he didn't. Claire was simultaneously happy and worried at his silence.

"Give me a moment."

"Okay, two minutes and then I'm sending Chloe over."

At the sound of the little girl's name, some of the fog lifted from Claire's brain and she waited to see how Aidan would react.

After about ten seconds, he released her. The loss of his heat almost seemed wrong.

Aidan pierced her with a stare. "She's gone."

She found her voice. "That's all well and good, but what now?"

"That is entirely up to you, Claire Davis. I only asked for a kiss, and while that was just a taste of what it would be like to be naked with a shifter, I won't touch you again until you ask me."

She opened her mouth and then promptly closed it. She really should tell him it would never happen, but that would be too final. A small part of her wanted more.

Aidan smoothed his hair. "Think about it. For now, I'll go over first. Come over once you've washed your face or Chloe will guess what happened here."

She narrowed her eyes. "Why, are you ashamed to kiss a human?"

"An hour ago, yes, I would've been. But now, shame is the furthest thing from my mind. I could lose myself in your mouth, Claire. Just imagine what would happen if I could taste your pussy, too."

With that, Aidan left.

Standing in the empty room, Claire lifted her fingers to her lips. No man had ever devoured her mouth as if he were starving. She would really need to think about what she wanted. More importantly, she'd have to decide if she could resist a particular cougar for an entire month.

If her pussy had anything to say about it, then the answer was no.

Shit. She had some serious thinking to do.

Chapter Seven

Only when Aidan sat down with his daughter to listen to what Dani had told her did both man and cougar cool down.

Kissing Claire had made his body burn in all the right places. Hell, he'd been close to coming just from her rubbing her belly against his cock.

He should feel guilty, but he couldn't. He'd been half dead for five years, yet tasting Claire's mouth made him feel alive again. While it made his cat happy, it scared the shit out of Aidan.

Chloe poked his arm with a finger. "Are you listening, Daddy?"

"Yes, baby, but I don't think sleeping outside Claire's door in cougar form is necessary. I know you're still learning, but I can shift quickly and then you can follow if I need your help."

Not that he ever planned to request his seven-year-old daughter's help against an intruder.

Chloe sighed, crumpled up her drawing of a cougar cub in front of a door, and tossed it aside. "Maybe I should use some of Dani's ideas instead."

"And what, exactly, did Dani tell you to try?"

His daughter shrugged. "Just to watch things. If I can't pay attention and focus, I'll never be as good as her or you."

Somehow, he guessed Dani had said more to his daughter. Before he could grill her, the door opened and Claire walked in.

Her hair was smoothed, her clothes righted, and the flush gone from her cheeks. No one, apart from maybe Kian or Dani, would ever guess what had transpired across the hallway.

A small part of him didn't like that.

Smiling, Claire walked over to the table and sat on the other side of Chloe, putting her opposite of Aidan. She never looked at him, but instead focused on Chloe. "So, do you have any ideas to help me?"

Chloe sighed again. "No. I keep trying, but Daddy says they aren't good ideas."

Claire glanced to him and back to Chloe. "Oh, he did, did he? Well, how about we take a break from planning and you ask me some questions while your father finds us something to eat."

Chloe looked to Aidan. "Oh, Daddy, can you make your specialty? It's been so long since we had enchiladas. Claire would like them."

He smiled. "Oh, Claire would like them, huh?" He tickled his daughter's side a second and she laughed. "I think you want them. If it were up to you, we'd have them every day."

Bright with laughter, Chloe looked to Claire. "You like them, don't you? Daddy really does make the best."

Claire smiled and looked at him with amusement in her eyes. The sight made his stomach flip. "I think it sounds like a great idea. I eat almost anything, except raw meat. I'm human, after all."

Aidan grinned. "Too bad, because they taste best with raw meat."

Chloe frowned. "Stop lying, Daddy. Enchiladas need cooked meat."

74

Both he and Claire laughed at the affront in Chloe's voice. As he met the human's gaze, a sense of rightness settled over him. It was almost as if they were acting like a family.

The thought made him pause. He barely knew the human, and she had important work to do. She wouldn't give it all up to live with him and be a stepmother to his daughter.

Claire must've noticed the change in his expression, because her smile disappeared, replaced with curiosity in her eyes. "Enchiladas sound great. I can look after Chloe if you need to retrieve ingredients." Claire looked to Chloe and winked. "I have my secondary bodyguard to protect me."

As Chloe beamed, some of the earlier ease returned to Aidan, although he was still hesitant to leave his daughter with a near stranger.

His cat, however, sent him thoughts of calm and trust. The human would look after their cub. If they asked one of the neighbors to keep an ear out, everything would be fine.

Only because Aidan lived in the heart of the soldiers' wing did he consider it.

Claire tapped her foot against his under the table. Meeting her gaze, her voice was soft. "I'll take good care of her, Aidan. I love working with children. However, if you would feel safer with another guard, you can send one if you like."

The human's tone was sincere and he didn't scent any deceit. He had no fucking idea what would happen between them in the future, if anything, but in this, both man and cat sensed she would do a good job.

Looking to Chloe, he asked, "Does that sound like a good plan, Chloe? Would you like to stay with Claire while I get the ingredients?"

She bobbed her head, her curls bouncing. "Yes. Then I can ask her most of my questions and you won't get bored."

He doubted he'd be bored at anything Claire Davis had to say since he then could maybe use it to persuade the human to give him another kiss. That wouldn't violate his declaration of her needing to ask him for more. It would still only be a kiss.

He tried not to think about why he wanted to kiss the human again.

Before his mind could relive the kiss from earlier, Aidan stood. "My cell number is on the fridge. We may be inside a mountain, but our techs installed something so we could use them. I'm going to have some of the neighboring soldiers listen for trouble, but call me the instant anything happens. Understood?"

The corner of Claire's mouth ticked up and she gave a mock salute. "Yes, captain."

Chloe whispered, "He's not a captain. Daddy's a head sentry."

Claire whispered back, "Thank you." She looked up at Aidan, humor dancing in her eyes. "Yes, head sentry."

He couldn't help but smile. "I'll be back in twenty minutes at the most." Glancing at his daughter, he laid a hand on her head. "Be good, baby, okay?"

"Of course, Daddy. Now, go so I can ask some questions. Claire might be shy and I don't want you to scare her."

To her credit, Claire merely bit her lip and remained silent. "Okay, okay, I'm leaving."

As he turned toward the door, Aidan took one last glance at Chloe and Claire. Their heads were together, Chloe whispering about how her daddy sometimes was too protective. Truth was his daughter was right. But his gut told him Claire would be good for his daughter. In what respect, he didn't know, but good for her somehow.

With that thought, he raced out the door and toward his neighbor's apartment. Even with his gut telling him Claire would take care of Chloe, both man and cat wanted to hear more of her voice. Maybe even breathe in more of her scent.

Yes, Aidan was in big fucking trouble.

~ ~ ~

A few minutes after Aidan left, Claire finished her answer about what humans did in school all day. With a mischievous look in her eyes, Chloe leaned closer. "Now that Daddy shouldn't be able to hear us, I have a very important question."

Claire wasn't sure she liked the sound of that. "What's your question, Chloe?"

"Well, I think my Daddy likes you. He's lonely. Will you be his friend?"

She blinked. "Why do you think he likes me?"

Chloe tapped her chin. "Well, he usually doesn't laugh with strangers. He also smells a little like you when usually he only smells of me and him. I think he hugged you earlier. He gives good hugs, and only to people he likes."

Well aware she was on dangerous ground, Claire was careful with her answer. "I think he laughed because you were here, Chloe. He didn't laugh with me when we were alone."

She frowned. "Well, if he was hugging you, then he wouldn't be laughing."

The child was closer to the truth than Claire liked. Time to steer the conversation away from her and Aidan. It was hard enough not reliving his kiss from earlier. "Your daddy seems nice, but his job is to protect me. I don't think he wants to be my friend."

Chloe studied her with amber eyes. Finally, she replied, "At least, try. Then maybe he will worry less about me. I love my daddy, but he's sad too often. He misses my mom."

The pain in Chloe's voice squeezed Claire's heart. She needed to lighten the mood, both for her sake and Chloe's.

An idea struck Claire, and she reached for some blank paper and pencils. Moving them in front of Chloe, she asked, "I know you want to ask me questions, but can I ask you one, too?"

Chloe tilted her head. "What?"

"I'm new here. What dangers should I look out for? I think we should make a list. That will help keep me out of trouble and make your job easier."

Nodding, Chloe picked up her pencil. "Good idea. Poachers are really bad people. Make sure to stay away from them."

She'd heard of illegal poachers, but had never bothered to look into the details. "Are there many?"

"Sometimes. But they killed my mom and baby brothers, so Daddy always wants me to be careful and not wander off."

Claire's heart skipped a beat. She forced her voice to remain light. "I didn't know you had any brothers."

"They were waiting to be born. I sometimes wish they were here so I could meet them."

Her idea to change the topic wasn't going well. Still, finding out Aidan had lost not only his mate, but his unborn children made her better understand Chloe's comments about his loneliness.

She would absolutely change the topic, but Claire had one more question. "How long ago were they taken?"

"I was really little, so I don't remember. But Daddy says five years. I know, because he always brings home flowers on that day."

"The day they died?" Chloe nodded and Claire continued. "Well, flowers should be enjoyed every day. How about we make some origami flowers for your dad? Do you think he'd like that?"

Chloe's eyes brightened. "My friend Jeff can make the cranes, but he's older. Can I really do it?"

Claire nodded. "I'll help you, but we need to hurry or your dad will walk in on the surprise."

"Okay, then show me."

As Claire helped Chloe make an origami flower, her mind wandered to all the little girl had revealed. Losing a mate was bad enough, but Aidan had also lost his unborn children. Her curiosity burned to know how, but she wasn't about to bring up the topic again with Chloe. The little girl was finally smiling again as she attempted to make a flower on her own.

Chloe's flower might look like a ball of crumpled paper, but if she were as stubborn at her father, she would get it right eventually.

Still, Claire wanted to help her finish the flowers on time, so she focused on folding and creasing the paper in just the right way. The rhythm and concentration helped her forget about Aidan and Chloe's tragic past.

They had six decent flowers made by the time Aidan returned. As soon he stepped inside, Chloe raced to her dad and jumped up and down in front of him. "Come see, Daddy. Me and Claire made you a surprise."

Aidan raised an eyebrow. "A surprise, eh?"

He met her eyes and Claire was careful not to let her features reflect her thoughts. "Yes, a surprise. Chloe, tell him to close his eyes and you can give it to him."

Chloe looked up at her dad. "Close your eyes and hold out your hands, Daddy, and hurry."

Setting down his bag of groceries, he smiled and closed his eyes. "Okay, what's my surprise?"

Racing back to the table, Chloe scooped up the flowers and went back to her dad. Gingerly, she placed the origami flowers into his hand. "Okay, open them!"

Aidan looked down at the paper flowers in his hand. "What are these?"

Chloe answered, "Paper flowers. Claire said we should have flowers every day not just once a year, so we made some."

Aidan met her eyes, but his expression was unreadable. He knew she knew about the death of his mate and unborn children.

Part of her want to demand more information, but she wouldn't do that to him or Chloe. At least, not at this time.

Still, Chloe was looking expectantly at her father, who was still silent. Claire raised her brows. "What do you think of the flowers, Aidan? Your daughter worked really hard on them."

Looking at his daughter, he crouched down and gave her a half-hug. "I love them, Chloe. You should teach me how to make them later."

Chloe nodded. "Of course." She pointed to the groceries. "But now you need to make dinner. I'm hungry and Claire wants your enchiladas, too."

Smiling, Claire added, "Chloe, dear, how about we make some more flowers while your dad makes dinner? Then we can decorate the table for dinner and make it special."

Aidan's daughter ran back to the table and sat next to Claire. Taking a sheet of paper, she asked sheepishly, "Can you help me again?"

After giving Aidan one last glance, she nodded at Chloe. As they made more origami flowers and Aidan started dinner, Claire decided she would ask Aidan about his mate and children the following day when Chloe was at school. Since she had a breakfast meeting with Kian, she'd have to do it beforehand. Bringing up the topic would be the hard part, but Claire needed to know the truth. Poachers had never been the focus of her organization, but if she could help raise awareness, she needed knowledge. Aidan could give it to her.

~~~

Thankfully, Chloe occupied Claire while Aidan made his open enchiladas. He was in no mood to laugh or smile.

Judging by the flowers Chloe had made him and her comment about needing them every day, Claire knew about how Aidan brought home flowers on the anniversary of his mate and unborn children's death.

It wasn't as if he could blame Chloe. The cub was a child, and for whatever reason, had taken a shine to Claire and didn't hold back.

Still, Claire knowing the full extent of his loss irked him. Emily's death was private and he rarely shared it with anyone.

The only saving grace was that the human hadn't looked at him with pity or sadness. Actually, her look of understanding had been much worse. She didn't know shit, but thought she did.

Chopping the tomatoes briskly eased some of his irritation. He at least had something to cool his cock if it started getting ideas again. To avoid Claire asking him questions, he was going to put distance back between them.

His cat didn't like that idea and pressed him to reconsider, but Aidan was the one in charge. The cougar would just have to deal with it.

A snarl reverberated inside his head. *The female could help their pain. Telling her the truth would help them to heal. Maybe then she would allow them to kiss her again.*

No more kissing, cougar.

"Look, Daddy. I made one all by myself."

Aidan turned toward his daughter, who held up a slightly crumpled flower. Her grin was infectious and all thoughts of putting distance between him and Claire vanished for the moment. "How many flowers do you have now?"

Chloe counted. "Seven."

"You have about thirty minutes until dinner is ready. Let's see how many you can make, okay?"

Nodding, Chloe reached for another piece of paper. Claire tried to catch his eye, but Aidan turned back around to finish making dinner.

Once the enchiladas were in the oven, he picked up his cell phone. "I'm going to check on Claire's clothes. I'll be in the bedroom if you need me."

Before either of the females could say a word, Aidan rushed into the bedroom and shut the door. Since Claire had yet to sleep in the room, it smelled only of laundry detergent and a little dust.

Dialing Dani's number, he let it ring. His sentry partner answered. "Hey Aidan, is something wrong?"

"No, but do you have a second?"

"Make it quick."

"Okay, I need to check on the status of clothes for Claire."

Dani paused before replying, "That anxious to get her out of yours, Aidan?"

He growled. "I still don't appreciate you doing that behind my back."

"Hey, it worked out for the best. You got to kiss her, after all."

Pushing aside the memory of Claire's soft lips, he answered, "It's not going to happen again, Dani, so just drop the teasing and stay out of my business."

"Listen, Aidan—"

Even though Dani couldn't see him, Aidan shook his head. "No, don't 'Listen, Aidan' me, Danika."

Dani growled, "Shut up, Aidan, and listen. It's about much more than you and you know it. Chloe needs a mother and she already adores Claire. That should convince you to at least give her a chance."

"Do I want to fuck Claire? Yes. Do I want to mate her? No. Chloe is happy and doesn't need to grow attached only to have someone else ripped from her side. She's been through enough."

"As have you. Think about it, Aidan. Claire will be safe on DarkStalker's land for a month, without the prying eyes of human law enforcement to try to arrest either one of you. That's plenty of time to see if she's maybe your second chance."

For a long time, Aidan had believed he would never have a second chance. Yet just hearing one of his clan members mentioning it put the idea into his head. While he'd never search out a mate just for himself, Dani had a point about Chloe needing a mother. Surely, Emily would've wanted him to find another for their daughter.

Aidan had no hopes of ever falling in love again. Lust was easy enough; hell, one whiff of Claire's female and lavender scent and he went hard as stone. But would lust be enough for someone like Claire?

Without realizing it, he said aloud, "I can't give any female love, Dani."

His friend was quiet for a second before she answered, "We all miss Emily, but she's gone, Aidan. She, more than anyone, would've told you to go after something you want. It's okay to want another female. Your heart is big enough for more than one shot at love."

Maybe, but he didn't want to talk about it anymore. Instead, he changed the subject. "I need to go, so just tell me when Claire will have some new clothes? She has a meeting with Kian tomorrow morning and she probably doesn't want to show up in my sweatpants."

"Someone is driving back from the nearest town with a few things and more will be delivered tomorrow. I'll have things sent as soon as they arrive. I need to go, but just think about it, Aidan. Claire has dedicated most of her adult life to helping shifters. She's nothing like the human poachers. She won't betray you."

The phone went dead and Aidan stared at the screen, hoping his dead mate would magically appear and tell him what to do.

His cougar knew what he wanted, though. A new mate wasn't a betrayal. A new mate would be a fresh start.

With a million thoughts racing through his head, a sudden knock on the door startled him. "Yes?"

"The kitchen timer beeped."

It was Claire. Exactly how long had she been standing there? Even with her paltry human hearing, the doors weren't soundproofed.

Since he wasn't about to drill her through the door, or at all about his phone conversation with Dani, Aidan crossed the room and opened the door. As Claire searched his eyes, he waited to see what she'd say. A small part of him was ashamed to think she heard about him wanting to fuck her but not mate her.

Why the hell am I worrying about it? All I've done is kiss her. With all the doubting and questioning, Aidan was starting to feel like a goddamn teenager again. He missed the days of knowing exactly where he stood with regards to females.

Claire raised an eyebrow. "Are you just going to stand here, stare at me, and let dinner burn? Some women may dance around the issue, but I'm hungry. I want the enchiladas I've heard so much about."

The human acting the same as before eased his worries. "If you would move out of the way, I could check on them."

Raising her chin, Claire moved aside and flourished her arm. "Excuse my human non-slenderness for blocking your path."

He moved his head toward her ear and whispered, "I don't mind your non-slenderness. I rather like it, but I was merely keeping my promise not to touch you unless you asked."

Claire blinked and his ego ticked up a notch. Quickly regaining her wits, she pointed toward the kitchen. "Just go check on dinner. I'm too hungry to keep arguing with you."

Grinning at his small win, Aidan moved past the human and went to check on the enchiladas. His doubts with Dani on the phone were nearly forgotten. He had no idea what the next day would bring, but for now, he was going to enjoy dinner with his daughter and a human who was fun to tease.

CHAPTER EIGHT

The next morning, Claire sipped her second cup of coffee and willed the fog to lift from her brain.

Even though dinner had been uneventful and Aidan and Chloe had left fairly early, she'd barely slept more than an hour or two. Every time she closed her eyes, either her kiss with Aidan or a reimagining of his mate's death played inside her mind. Since the man had been close-lipped during dinner, it'd been up to her and Chloe to keep the conversation going. Or, rather, up to Chloe.

Remembering the little girl jumping from one topic to another made Claire smile. The girl was about as different from her father as could be. She must take after her mother.

Yet Chloe didn't even remember her mother. Even though Claire's parents had died a few years ago in a boating accident, she'd had twenty-eight years with them. She only hoped Chloe would have a mother some day and make new memories.

A small part of her wanted to be that person, but as much as she'd fallen in love with Chloe Scott, Claire had six more months of putting her work and the rights of others above her desires and wants. She'd worked too hard for too long to just give it all up.

Of course, by November, Aidan would probably have found someone else. At the thought of a tall, muscled shifter female hanging on his arm, she clenched her coffee mug in her fingers.

Before she could dwell too much on her reaction, a knock on the door brought her out of her thoughts. Moving to the door, she asked, "Who is it?"

"Aidan."

Opening the door, she put on an unassuming smile. "Good morning, enchilada master."

"I was hoping without Chloe, that name wouldn't stick."

She motioned with her head for him to come in. "You should wear it with pride. If your head sentry gig doesn't work out, you can always fall back on your culinary skills. I'm sure you could open a seasonal restaurant for the tourists who hike the nearby trails." Grunting, Aidan walked past her and she noticed the box. "What's inside there? Did my clothes finally get here?"

He raised an eyebrow. "Stop calling me enchilada master and I'll tell you."

She rolled her eyes. "Fine. If it means I can wear clothes my own size again, then I think I can manage that."

After placing it on the table, he moved to the couch and sat down. "Your meeting with Kian starts in twenty minutes. I'd hurry if I were you."

So, that was the way it was going to be then, as if they hadn't teased and even kissed the night before.

Since her meeting was too important to fuck up, Claire picked up the box and stopped at the entrance to the bathroom. Still, she could resist teasing the shifter male. "I'm locking the door, so don't try to peek."

Aidan merely waved a hand in dismissal. Irritated, Claire left him alone to get ready. Why his actions stung, she had no idea, but she refused to dwell on the feeling. Once she was done with her meeting and could touch base with her people at the SEA, she could focus back on her work and forget about Aidan Scott, his sexy kisses, and his adorable daughter. He clearly was no longer interested in her.

~~~

Aidan settled down to Claire's right, across from Kian and his mate, Trinity. While his and Claire's walk to the meeting spot had been in silence, the damn female had teased him the whole way here with her body.

No doubt, Dani had played a part in picking out the tight jeans and sweater that kept falling off Claire's shoulder. More than once, he'd peeked at her shapely ass. The real restraint had come when another male had stared at the exposed skin of her shoulder. Aidan's nails had dug hard enough into his palm to draw blood.

However, the meeting should distract him. Once Kian gave Claire her list of tasks, she would be too busy to tease him with either her words or her body. She clearly hadn't taken his hint of silence the night before. It seemed the female was determined to treat him as if she'd never heard about his past or possibly his comments on the phone with Dani.

He was about to frown in Claire's direction for the havoc she was bringing to his life when Trinity spoke up. "Enjoying your assignment, Aidan?"

If Dani had said anything to Trinity, then Aidan would hunt down his friend and kill her. "Chloe's helping me, so it's been fun." His cat urged him to look in Claire's direction, but Aidan resisted. "But my assignment isn't the purpose of this meeting, as you know, Trinity. Stop stalling and give Claire something to do."

Claire's voice was light. "Oh, I don't know, making origami flowers with Chloe is pretty fun. We could make enough to decorate the whole soldier's wing."

He did look at her then, with a deep frown. "I don't think so."

Claire raised her brows. "Have you asked all the soldiers if they'd mind?"

His frown deepened. "That's not the point. It's not going to happen, end of story."

Kian cleared his throat. If not for his training, Aidan's cheeks would've flushed.

Once both he and Claire looked in Kian's direction, Kian said, "While I wish I could spare Claire to make flowers with your daughter, Aidan, I'm afraid that's going to have to wait." Kian looked to Claire. "A secure internet connection has been set-up, but before I allow you to contact your people, I want to know more of what you expect from me. After that, I'll assign your first set of tasks with DarkStalker."

Claire would've made a comment for sure about the word 'allow' if Aidan had said it, but she didn't so much as blink an eye when Kian used it. Instead, she merely jumped right into business. "While my end goal is to record ads for TV and radio to use in the final two months leading up to the vote on the ballot, I think we should start small. The first statement from you and your clan will be the most important. It will set the tone for the entire campaign."

Kian merely leaned back in his chair. "Go on."

"I think you should issue a press release through my organization, stating your support. Nothing too exact, but enough to catch the public and media's notice. You can draft it yourself or I can do it, but either way, I want to tweak it before it goes live.

Of course, once it does go live, there's no turning back. I know you've had trouble with Human Purity in recent months. Their attacks might grow bolder after this."

Kian shrugged. "They're always waiting to attack, but I won't live in fear of them. The second I do, they've won. I trust Aidan and Dani to protect the clan."

Claire added, "I expected as much. If possible, I'd like the draft by this afternoon. With only six months to go, I don't want to waste another day."

Kian nodded. "I'll start on it straight away, but I think we should stagger GreyFire's support. That will give us more coverage on the news."

Claire smiled. "You claim not to know much about organizing with humans, but I think you're savvier than you realize."

Kian waved a hand. "Being clan leader for more than a decade has taught me a few things. Dealing with other clans is not as easy as you might expect."

As Kian studied Claire, Aidan's inner cougar growled. The male had a mate. He shouldn't be looking at their female.

Before Aidan could tell his cat that Claire didn't belong to them, Kian's voice filled the small conference room again. "Now, it's time to talk about your assignment. I want near-daily meetings with me and my staff, starting in three days' time. Until then, I will give you time to reshuffle events and meetings with your own people, provided you spent a portion of each day typing up tips, contacts, and lessons learned that I can use."

Claire leaned on her elbows on the table. "If you expect me to give up all of my contacts, then you're crazy."

As Kian remained silent, Aidan felt a sense of pride. His female may be human, but she was an alpha in her own right.

Wait, why am I calling her mine?

His cat purred. Because she was.

Before he could do more than think the word "fuck," Kian answered, "Fair enough, but I need some contacts and letters of introduction. That is one of the requirements for me to help with your campaign."

As Claire stared back at Kian, Aidan noticed Trinity staring at him. Considering the shifter female's penchant for interrupting, she was being unusually quiet. It was no secret among the DarkStalker clan that Trinity Perez-Murray was Kian's right-hand helper. When Kian had been recovering from his bout with a rabid bear-shifter the previous year, she and Kian's brother, Sy, had kept the clan together.

What the fuck is Trinity up to?

Claire's voice interrupted his musings. "I will introduce you to a few of my contacts at a time so I can judge how they, and you, will handle it. I'm sure you can understand my caution given that these people are largely responsible for the marriage vote being on the ballot in the first place. Without their resources and support, I never would've collected enough signatures."

Kian replied, "That I can live with." Kian looked to Aidan. "Hector will be by in an hour with Claire's laptop. He'll set up the connection."

Hector Martinez was a much sought-after young male in DarkStalker. While Hector was oblivious, every single female in the clan went out of her way to attract his attention.

And that male was going to be in the same room as Claire for who the hell knew how long. Only by gripping his thigh under the table was Aidan able to resist a growl. Not trusting himself to speak, he merely nodded.

Kian studied him a second before looking back to Claire. "We'll meet again tomorrow. If you could bring whatever you've typed up by then, I'd appreciate it. I'll have the press release sent to you by three p.m."

DarkStalker's leader stood up, and everyone else followed suit. Reaching out a hand, Claire smiled. "I think we're still circling each other, as you put it yesterday, but I think eventually we'll establish an equal footing."

Kian shook Claire's hand and then dropped it. "I think we will. Your help will truly make a difference here, Claire Davis."

"I hope so."

After a few more goodbyes, Aidan motioned for Claire to leave. Not trusting himself to touch her, he kept his distance the entire way back to her apartment.

~ ~ ~

Even without touching her, Claire felt the heat and tension radiating off Aidan's body. She may not be a shifter with super senses, but even she could tell his mood was off. The man's jerky movements and refusal to acknowledge her presence was unlike any other time she'd walked beside him. At least, since the very first time when he'd been naked in the snow.

Why he was in a foul mood, she had no fucking idea. The meeting with Kian had gone as expected, and she'd held her ground. If Aidan was upset with her for standing up to DarkStalker's leader, well, tough. Her organization was like her clan, and she was damn well going to protect them.

They arrived at her door. She reached for the handle, but Aidan beat her to it and whispered, "Let me go in first to check."

Aware ears could be listening, she merely motioned for him to go ahead. The sooner they entered her place, the sooner she could find out the cause of Aidan's tension. The broody looks and stiff posture needed to go back to the ease and laughter of yesterday. That was the shifter she wanted to act as her guard.

Aidan cracked the door, waited, and then crept inside. After about thirty seconds, he ordered, "Come inside."

With a sigh, she entered her place and headed for the kitchen. The buzz from her coffee was wearing off and she needed something to eat before dealing with the rest of the day, let alone before standing up to a two-hundred-pound-plus shifter male.

Yet as she opened the refrigerator door, she felt Aidan's gaze on her back. Tired of his mood, food would just have to wait. She turned around. "What do you want?"

"Nothing."

Shutting the refrigerator, she strode toward him and poked him in the chest. "What the hell is up with you? And don't say nothing, because that's a lie."

He stared a second before growling, "Hector's coming."

She blinked. "The computer guy? What does he have to do with anything?"

Aidan took a step closer. Only a few inches separated their bodies. His voice was low when he answered, "Every female wants him in their bed. You will, too."

She frowned. "What the hell, Aidan? You'd better start explaining or I'll call Dani and have her make sense of it all."

Leaning toward her, Claire took a step back, which only elicited another growl from Aidan. He was still close enough that she could feel the heat of his body when he answered, "If you flirt

94

with him, my cat will urge me to beat the living shit out of him, so keep your distance."

"You've clearly gone insane, especially since all morning you've acted like yesterday never happened. Now you're jealous? I'm tired of wondering and guessing, Aidan Scott. Tell me straight what's going on here or I will request another guard."

In the blink of an eye, Aidan drew her up against his body, warmth and awareness flaring everywhere their bodies touched. Heat and glowing cougar eyes replaced the irritation in Aidan's gaze. His breath was hot against her face as he murmured, "You won't request another guard."

She cleared her throat. "Why?"

Nuzzling her cheek, he whispered, "Because you are mine."

As Aidan hauled her tighter against his body, Claire stopped breathing. Being surrounded by Aidan's heat and scent of male and forest was making it hard to think. All he had to do was kiss her and Claire would forget reason and act on her hormones.

Mustering up what logic she still possessed, she asked, "How is that possible, Aidan? One minute you're laughing with me, yet the next you pretend like I don't exist. If that's how the next month is going to be, I can't do it."

His voice was low and gravelly. "So you admit to wanting me, too."

Claire pushed gently against his chest until she could look into his glowing amber eyes. "Being attracted to you is one thing, but we both have reasons why it can't happen, and you know it."

"Forget tomorrow or the next month. If you want me, then tell me, Claire. Otherwise you will have to find yourself another guard because all my inner cougar can think about is getting you naked and covering you in my scent." He squeezed her waist. "It's been a long time since I've wanted a female this badly. I'm done pretending. Say the word, and I'll have you forgetting all other males. You'll only think of me."

Claire searched his eyes. She wanted nothing more than to allow Aidan to explore and scent her body. However, politics were never that simple. For better or for worse, every decision in her life revolved around political outcomes and strategies.

Could she really keep something such as sleeping with Aidan from the media? If anything leaked out to the press, both her and her campaign would be finished.

Or, so she'd assumed thus far. Truth be told, Claire had never run numbers or polls to see if her being with a shifter long-term would hurt her chances. She'd already garnered most of the political support she needed for her campaign; all that was left was to convince the voters of her cause. With them, bias could be justified if she were fighting to get married herself. After all, everyone loved a taboo love story.

Whoa, wait a second. She only met Aidan yesterday. Despite how right it felt in his arms, she barely knew him.

Could she really go through with it and jeopardize everything she'd accomplish just to be with a shifter male?

Of course, if she slept with him once, she might have a better idea if it was worth pursuing the idea of different tactics and eventually marrying a shifter. If sleeping with Aidan ended up being nothing but lust that faded after sex, she could pretend this one time never happened. No one would know. Or, at least, no one who would ever share her secret. She trusted Kian to keep his clan in line.

Either way, she needed more data to make a final decision. To do that, she needed to experience more than just kisses; she needed to get naked with Aidan Scott.

Before she could change her mind, she asked, "How long before Hector will be here?"

Aidan's eyes flashed at the other man's name. "About an hour, why?"

Ignoring the thundering heartbeat in her ears, Claire gathered her courage and tilted up her head. "Then make that hour count, Aidan."

He growled. "Once I start, I won't be able to stop."

Running a hand up his chest, she paused where his neck met his shoulder to strum her thumb against him. "Since I'm on birth control and shifters don't carry STDs or other diseases humans can catch, do whatever you wish with me, Aidan. I'm giving you permission."

CHAPTER NINE

Not wanting Claire to change her mind, both man and cat growled as he lowered his lips to hers. The instant his tongue met hers, the urge to be inside her grew stronger.

Exploring the inside of her mouth, Aidan moved his hands to her ass and lifted, pressing his human against his straining cock. Her moans made his dick pulse.

Fuck. He needed to get them naked.

After Claire wrapped her legs around his waist, he never stopped exploring her mouth as he slowly walked to the bedroom. When they were close enough to the mattress, he broke the kiss to lay Claire down.

The sight of her slightly swollen lips made his cougar happy, but it wasn't enough. They needed access to her body. The more they scented her, the more others would stay away from their female.

Running a hand up Claire's belly, between her breasts, and then to the side of her face, he murmured, "Beautiful," before gently removing her glasses. Folding them up, he took a few steps back. At Claire's sound of protest, he smiled. "Unless you want your glasses smashed, give me a second."

"Then hurry up because right now, you're blurry and I want to see you."

Laying her glasses down on the dresser, he turned and tore off his shirt. Once he was close enough, Claire's gaze moved to his bared chest. She'd seen him naked before, but this time was different. Aidan wasn't a young man of twenty any more, but nearly twice that age. Would a few gray hairs on his chest deter her?

Judging by the hungry look in her eyes, the answer was no. Then her eyes moved to the bulge in his jeans. Her voice was husky. "Show me all of you and come closer. I want a proper look, not a half-blurry version."

He liked that she wasn't afraid to ask for what she wanted. That should make things interesting in bed later on.

Unbuttoning his jeans, Aidan kicked off his shoes first, then his pants and boxers. He moved to the foot of the bed and Claire's eyes on his cock forced out a drop of precum.

His cougar snarled. Why did she still have clothes on?

Running his hands up Claire's plump thighs, he stopped at the hem of her sweater and ran one finger underneath, against her skin. Claire sucked in her breath and he murmured, "Now it's your turn. You can do it yourself, or you can let me undress you."

The corner of her mouth ticked up. "I think I like the idea of you trying to undress me."

"Try? Human, I bet I can make you beg for my cock by the time I have you naked."

"Oh, really? I'd like to see that."

"Challenge accepted; although just know I'm going to take my time."

Claire opened her mouth to reply, but Aidan ran his hands under her sweater to rub her belly and sides in slow, deliberate movements. He was careful to avoid her breasts. He hadn't lied; she would be begging when he was done.

Moving his hands back to the waist of her jeans, he undid the top button, leaned down and kissed the skin it revealed. Flicking his tongue, Claire wiggled under his touch. Smiling, he blew on her wet skin and the scent of her arousal grew stronger.

Unzipping her fly, he whispered, "You're wet now, but I want you drenched. I think I need to tease you some more. Raise your hips for me."

Claire obeyed for once, and he slid her jeans down. Slipping off her shoes, he tugged them free. At the sight of her creamy skin, he leaned down and nibbled her inner thigh, working his way up to the crease of her panties. So close to her pussy, he breathed deeply, both man and cat desperate to brand her scent into their memory.

Breathing wasn't enough, and moving aside the strip of material, Aidan gave a long lick up her slit, stopping just short of her clit. Needing another taste, he did it again, savoring his female's honey.

Claire grabbed his hair and wiggled her hips. With a chuckle, he backed off only to see Claire staring at him with narrowed eyes. Her voice dripped with frustration. "We have less than an hour. You'd better speed up the process or you'll never get the chance to fuck me."

He winked. "I told you I'd have you begging by the time you were naked. Actually, you're begging already and I'm only half done."

Claire huffed. "I'm done waiting." She sat up. "If you don't hurry up, I'm going to leave your dick hard and aching. You'll have to take care of yourself then."

Taking the hem of her sweater, he tugged it up and she lifted her arms. He tossed it to the side. "If you want it hard and fast, then I can do that." Before she could reply, he tugged her bra down to reveal her full, beautiful breasts. Rolling one hard nipple, Claire bit her lip to keep from groaning. "You have five seconds to remove your bra and panties or I rip them off. One, two..."

~~~

Not that Claire wanted to admit it, but the damn shifter had kept his promise to make her all but beg. Never had being undressed turned her on so much in her life.

Granted, most of the men she'd been with had been more interested in getting their dick inside her and finding their own orgasm, than helping along hers.

Aidan, on the other hand, had nearly made her come with most of her clothes still on.

As he started counting, Claire didn't waste a second slipping her bra straps off and unhooking it. A good bra was hard to find and she wasn't about to destroy it, not even for possible mind-blowing shifter sex.

Her underwear didn't have a chance, however, because the instant Aidan reached five, he extended a claw and sliced them off.

She didn't have a second to scold him, let alone wonder if he found her as attractive naked as he did clothed, because he pushed her down on the bed and covered his hard, hot body over hers.

His weight, size, and chest hairs teasing her nipples made her feel feminine in a way she hadn't felt in years.

Aidan moved a knee between her legs and pressed against her. She cried out and Aidan's look grew pleased. "I wanted to lick you nice and slowly, building the anticipation, but my little human is impatient. I'm going to fuck you now, in the way I've been imagining since yesterday."

Lowering his head to kiss her, she felt his hand between her legs, teasing her pussy. Then the next second, his long, hard cock was deep inside her. Aidan's kiss muffled her cries.

Instead of hammering away, he remained still, allowing her to acclimate to his size. And, damn, what a size. She was almost too full, but knew it would be delicious when he finally moved.

Aidan broke the kiss, took her wrists, and pinned them above her head. The combination of his tender strength and the amber glow of his eyes only made her wetter. This was really happening. She was about to have sex with a shifter.

Before doubts could set in about the enormity of the situation, Aidan pulled out and thrust slowly. After a few deep movements, he tightened his grip on her wrists and took a nipple into his mouth. The wet heat of his tongue circling her sensitive skin made her moan, but then he bit her and she screamed.

She was so close already. All he would have to do was bite her nipple again and she'd come.

But he released her nipple with a pop and stared into her eyes as he moved out and then pounded back into her pussy. Increasing his pace, her whole body moved with his efforts.

Aidan wasn't merely fucking her. No, he was claiming her body.

Changing his angle, she moaned. Thank fuck the walls were made out of stone so the neighbors couldn't hear her.

She closed her eyes to focus on the building pressure, but Aidan stopped and ordered, "Open your eyes. I want to see you come."

Unable to resist the dominance in his voice, she obeyed. The second her eyes met his glowing amber ones, Aidan moved again, only faster.

In the past, she'd always been fairly quiet during sex. This time, however, she couldn't help but say, "Harder, Aidan. Don't hold back."

With a growl, he complied. Only because he held her wrists did she not move up against the headboard.

His voice thick and heavy, he stated, "My human. Only mine."

Without thinking, she answered, "Yes."

Maneuvering her wrists into one of his strong hands, he glided down her neck, her chest, her belly, and finally her clit. After a few flicks, he pressed his thumb against her hard nub and her orgasm hit, sending pleasure through her body. As her pussy clenched Aidan's cock, lights danced before her eyes.

Yet as much as she enjoyed the best orgasm of her life, she wanted more. She wanted Aidan to come inside her.

As if reading her mind, Aidan stilled. With a shout, he came. Unlike with a human, she could actually feel each hot spurt inside her body, branding his scent into her.

When the tension eased from Aidan's body, he melted on top of her and rolled to his side. Squeezing her close, Claire snuggled into his chest. A sense of safety and rightness settled over her, but she wondered if it would last.

Pushing her doubts about what would happen ten or twenty minutes from this moment, Claire breathed deeply and nuzzled Aidan's warm, slightly sweaty body. She wanted to memorize every single detail, from Aidan's warmth to the sound of his beating heart,, just in case this was all they had.

After all, Aidan has his work and his daughter, while Claire had her work and her mission. Even if Aidan wanted more, it probably wouldn't work. Something would leak to the press and the only way she could keep a shifter and have her vote pass in November was to marry one, and that wasn't happening any time soon.

Claire was in over her head. For all her years of strategizing and playing politics, she hadn't the faintest idea of what to do next.

~~~

As Aidan stroked Claire's soft hair, his inner cougar purred. Their female was at their side, just as she should always be.

The day before, Aidan would have argued the point. In that moment, with his sassy, smart female nuzzling his chest, he agreed with his cat.

The thought nearly made him frown. Man and cat might want the human, but did the human want him in the same way? Not only that, Aidan had his daughter to think of.

Chloe already loved Claire, but he wasn't about to give his daughter false hope. While bubbly on the outside, his daughter could be stoic on the inside. He knew she yearned for a mother. If she grew even closer to his human and then Claire left at the end of the month, it would devastate his daughter.

Not only that, but the vote in November was important to his entire clan. He needed to figure out a way to keep Claire Davis and pass human-shifter equality. What had once seemed like a good idea for others had become personal. Fool that he was, he saw himself keeping Claire forever. Hell, maybe even taking her as his mate.

Before he started thinking of all the reasons why that was fucking ridiculous, Claire's soft, sexy voice interrupted his thoughts. "I think we have time for one more go, but this time, I want to be on top."

Shifter males were dominant for the most part, yet the image of Claire riding his cock and him at her complete mercy already had his dick growing hard again.

He rolled his body until Claire was laying on his chest. Pushing herself up, heat danced in her eyes. "I'm going to take that as a yes."

Growling, he caressed her ass. "That's a hell yes, but you'd better get started."

Picking up the bed sheet, Claire cleaned between her legs and tossed the material away. With a wicked smile, she grabbed his cock with her soft hands and squeezed. As he sucked in a breath, she murmured, "Just checking you're ready."

When she tightened her hands around his cock again, he gripped her ass cheeks and then slapped one. His female squeaked and he chuckled as he slapped her other cheek. The heat in her eyes told him she liked it. "Just making sure you're ready, too."

Claire smiled a little too sweetly. "Just remember, payback is a bitch."

"Then, my human, game on. I will always win in the bedroom."

As Claire guided his cock inside her pussy, she clenched and he barely resisted a moan. Her voice was husky as she answered, "We'll see about that, Aidan Scott. I somehow think I can turn you into putty in my hands."

And true to her word, Claire Davis did exactly that.

CHAPTER TEN

An hour later, Claire resisted looking over at Aidan. They'd already shared half a dozen glances since Hector had arrived to set up her secure, tamper-proof Wi-Fi access. Any more looks and Hector would guess what had happened between her and Aidan right before Hector had arrived.

Much to Aidan's grumpy displeasure, they had both showered separately and changed clothes. The sheets and everything else, which hinted at their encounter in the bedroom, had been stashed in Aidan's apartment. Shifter senses were sensitive, but Claire was hoping the scented candles had been the last touch needed to hide it.

Not that she wanted to hide what she and Aidan had done because, damn, all she could think about was jumping back into bed with the cougar-shifter. Dominant one minute, and then teasing the next. If only he'd act that way always.

Hector snapped his fingers, turned, and smiled at Claire. His white teeth against his deeply tanned skin only enhanced the man's sexiness. "All set up, tested, and double-checked. I think that might be a new record for me."

Claire smiled back at Hector. "Thanks. Living without the internet just isn't possible for me anymore. You're sure no one can hack my access or my computer?"

Hector stood and took a step toward her. Even without looking at Aidan, she could feel his eyes on her.

Ignoring him, she focused on Hector, who answered, "Our security was greatly upgraded a few months ago. Only highly experienced hackers or high-powered government agencies could break through. I'm guessing you don't have any of them after you, right?" He lowered his voice to a whisper. "You can tell me if they are and I won't tell a soul."

Claire resisted a blink. Three days ago, she would've flirted back with Hector the cougar-shifter. Tall, teasing, and warm, he would've been her dream man. But it wasn't three days ago, and if she didn't usher the shifter out, Aidan would end up punching the man in the face. Claire may never have dated a shifter before, but she'd done her research and had several shifter contacts in the city. To say they overreacted when it came to their girlfriends or boyfriends would be an understatement.

Of course, Claire wasn't anyone's girlfriend for the moment. Still, Hector had helped her and she didn't want him to leave with a broken nose or worse.

She whispered back, "No, I'm just a boring organizer." Raising her voice back to normal volume, she continued, "And this boring organizer has a lot of work to catch up on. Thanks for your help, but I'd really like to get started."

Hector bobbed his head. "No worries. But if you have even the slightest trouble or have a computer question, I left my phone number next to your laptop. Call me anytime."

Just the fact yet another shifter male was interested in her warmed her heart. "I will. Thanks again."

Hector gave a mock salute and then waved to Aidan. "See you later, Aidan."

After Aidan grunted in parting, Hector shook his head and left.

Alone, she frowned over at Aidan. "So you're grumpy with more than just me."

Between one beat and the next, Aidan had her cornered against the wall, his breath hot on her face. "Considering I wanted to punch his teeth out, I would say I did pretty well."

She poked his chest. "Don't go all alpha shifter on me. I may need Hector's help again if something goes wrong with the internet."

"He was flirting with you."

Raising an eyebrow, she smiled. "You're jealous."

A grunt was all the reply she received.

Laughing, she pushed playfully against Aidan's chest. "That's sweet in a weird way, but I have work to do."

"Give me a kiss first."

Staring up into Aidan's eyes, she searched his gaze. While there was heat and desire, she didn't see anything else. Before she could think better of it, she blurted out, "And what happens when Chloe gets home from school? Are you going to pretend none of this ever happened?"

For a second, he said nothing. Then he laid his forehead against hers and let out a sigh. "I don't know."

A lesser person might push Aidan away and take offense, but Claire understood what he meant. "I'm not expecting you to kiss and hold me in front of your daughter today or even next week. But while the 'where is this going' conversation can usually wait, I'm not a usual person. I always have to think three steps ahead, especially with the vote in November. If you want out, that's fine, but I need you to tell me directly."

Lifting his head, Aidan cupped her cheeks and strummed his thumbs against her skin. He simply stared into her eyes for a solid minute, as if he could read his future in her gaze. Finally, his voice was low when he replied, "Let's try for the month you're here and see how it goes."

While she still didn't have a plan for what to do if it worked out with her shifter, a little of the worry eased from her heart at the fact he wanted to try. "So, we keep it secret?"

Aidan moved one of his thumbs from her cheek to her lower lip. It took everything she had to concentrate on his words. "For now. Dani will guess, as will Kian and Trinity. But I want to try. For reasons I can't explain, I feel alive when I'm with you, Claire Davis, and I don't want to go back to being half-dead."

She stopped breathing a second. Careful to keep her tone even, she whispered, "You make me feel alive, too, Aidan Scott. Now, give me a kiss so I can get to work." As he hauled her against his body, she added, "Just a kiss. Kian is expecting information tomorrow, and I need to type something before his press release is delivered. Not to mention I need to contact Ryan, my second-in-command, and rearrange my schedule. So I mean it when I say just a kiss, okay?"

One corner of his mouth lifted and it made her heart warm. "In all my years of being a DarkStalker soldier, merely kissing you and letting you go will be one of the hardest things I've ever done."

Before she could reply, he kissed her.

Wrapping her arms around his broad back, each stroke of his tongue only made her melt a little more against him. When he finally broke the kiss, her brain and her pussy had different ideas of what she should do next.

Aidan made the decision by releasing her and stepping away. She wanted to shout for him to do more than kiss her, but merely cleared her throat instead. "While I'm working, maybe you can think of what to make for dinner."

He raised an eyebrow. "Do I look like your personal servant?"

Giving him a slow once-over, she nodded. "Yes, I think you are."

Mischief flashed in his eyes. "For that, just know I'm going to plan in my head every way I want to take you tonight when Chloe spends the night with my brother."

"With your brother?"

"Yes, because I have some very important duties to attend to tonight." He lowered his voice to a husky whisper. "And just know that I was holding back earlier. Get ready, human, because I'm going to take you the shifter way later tonight."

With that, Aidan turned and walked into the kitchen. She followed his fine ass until it was hidden by the counter. With a sigh, she went to her laptop and opened a new document. It was barely noon, which meant she had hours to think of just what "the shifter way" entailed.

The responsible thing to do was think of solutions where she could both pass shifter equality and date a shifter. But Claire took the easy way out and began typing information for Kian. Planning three steps ahead could happen tomorrow. She could afford to live in the moment for a day.

~~~

Right before Chloe was due to return from school, Aidan took a cold shower.

110

Watching Claire for hours without being able to touch her had nearly killed him. His cock had been hard almost all afternoon, straining against his jeans, urging him to pick her up and fuck her against the wall.

Yet his human half won out, understanding her need to work. In a way, listening to her give orders and change strategies with her second-in-command had made Aidan want her all the more. She may not direct men and women in battle, but she was a commander in her own right. If she'd been a shifter, Claire Davis would've been an alpha lioness.

When Kian's press release arrived, she ended her phone call and worked in silence. At least, when she'd been on the phone, Aidan could pretend to be working while he listened to her voice. While man and cat hoped to one-day share a comfortable silence with Claire, their connection was new. Aidan wanted to pick apart her brain and then take her to bed and make her scream. All the silence did was taunt him.

Turning the knob to make the shower cooler, he pushed thoughts of Claire aside. His daughter would be home soon, which meant no touching Claire until his brother stopped by to pick up Chloe. The self-enforced no touching rule would ensure Claire and Chloe had time to bond. After all these years, his daughter deserved a mother-like figure. That meant Aidan needed to share Claire Davis, especially if they were to have a future someday.

His cat growled. Of course, they would have a future with her. She was their female.

Rather than argue, he stepped out of the shower and dressed. Then Aidan headed to the living room, where he found Dani standing with a grim expression and Claire looking puzzled. *Fuck, what happened now?* He asked, "What's going on?"

111

Claire beat Dani to say, "I don't know. Dani said we had to wait until you showed up, so I've been sitting here thinking the worst."

He looked to his friend. "Well, I'm here now, so tell us what's up."

Dani nodded toward the couch. "I think you'd better sit down."

Her tone was commanding, which meant something serious had happened.

Obeying, Aidan sat next to Claire. "I'm sitting. Now, tell me straight what's going on."

Dani sighed. "Human Purity has released something to the media."

He frowned. "And what of it? They do that all the time, but most of it is bullshit."

"Not this time," Dani said. "I don't know how they did it, but they released a photo." She took out the tablet she had under her arm, swiped across the face, and turned it toward them. "Look for yourself."

The picture showed him standing naked in the snow across from Claire. Her face was turned toward the camera, her cheeks flushed from both the cold and her irritation with him. Across the bottom was a caption, "Shifter Equality Alliance President Claire Davis and her shifter lover."

Claire's groan garnered his attention. Looking at her with her head in her hands, he wanted to rub her back but resisted. Instead, he looked back to Dani and switched into head sentry mode. "Where did this come from?"

Dani turned off the tablet. "One of the online tabloids picked it up first, and it's slowly gaining traction at all the other local media stations. *KOMO* and *KIRO News* have it on their online sites. No word about the *Seattle Times*, but if they can verify the source, they may run with it too."

Claire finally spoke. "The *Seattle Times* has been on the shifter marriage equality side for months now. I might be able to tap my contacts and start damage control. But…"

Aidan looked to Claire. "But, what?"

She met his gaze head-on with determination in her eyes. "You and I need to talk in private."

Sensing the command in her voice, he didn't argue. Looking to Dani, he instructed, "Pick Chloe up from school and take her to my brother's. After that, we need to set up a meeting with Kian. Let me know when, and Claire and I will be there after our talk."

While Dani may like to tease him, the situation was too serious to waste time. She merely nodded and walked to the door. "Keep your phone close. I should have a meeting put together in about half an hour."

Once she was gone, Aidan turned toward Claire. "I can see the wheels in your head turning. We don't have a lot of time, Claire, so tell me what you have planned."

~ ~ ~

Claire's greatest fear had materialized; she was the focus of a possible scandal.

What irritated her was the fact the photo had been taken before she'd ever kissed Aidan, let alone slept with him. If she hadn't, then what she was about to say would seem a lot crazier. Hell, she might not have had the nerve.

But they had slept together and even agreed to give their connection a chance. That might make things easier, 'might' being the key word.

Not backing down, she took a deep breath and spit out, "There is only one way to possibly turn this so-called scandal into something positive and still have the vote pass, but it will require changing your life dramatically."

He studied her a second before finally asking, "How can we save the situation?"

Despite her forced calm exterior, Claire's heart thumped inside her chest. She had expected to have a month to figure out her future, but thanks to one rogue photo, she would have to decide it right this second without any proof or reports to back up her decision. While she trusted her gut, her idea was risky at best and dangerous at worst.

Aidan ran a finger down her cheek and his touch helped ease her nerves. He murmured, "Just tell me, Claire. Patience isn't one of my strong suits. I may start growling if you don't start talking."

She gave a weak smile at his attempt to tease. The act helped strengthen her resolve. "If we tell the press we're engaged, the story could be turned into a positive. I don't know for sure since I haven't run any polls, but the news may actually help the campaign. If nothing else, it will turn the scandal into a love story, and the public always adores a good love story. My only concern would be if Trinity's earlier comments about the authorities staying away would continue or not. If not, we would have to hide."

Aidan was quiet for a few seconds. When he replied, his voice was quiet, "You've thought about this outcome in advance, haven't you?"

114

"I always think of possible outcomes in advance. It's my job."

"But the bigger question is if you planned it."

She narrowed her eyes. "No, and if you accuse me of that again, I will find someone who looks like you to stand in as my fiancé until after the vote in November."

His eyes flashing amber, he leaned closer. "No other male is going to put his hands on you."

"That still isn't an answer, Aidan."

Grunting, he moved closer until his knee touched hers. Taking her chin in his fingers, his voice was like steel. "I will be the one standing in as your fiancé."

The possessiveness of his tone made her shiver. Since she was headstrong, Claire had never been a woman who thought she wanted a dominant male, but she was starting to like it.

Keeping her tone even, she pushed. "That's only part of it. Do you think I planned this?"

He searched her eyes before leaning a hair's breadth from her lips, his breath hot against her skin. "No, Claire, I don't. Given your resistance at first, I think your attraction to me was unplanned. I also think your connection to Chloe is genuine. However, that still leaves the problem of Human Purity sneaking onto my clan's land and waiting for a photo op like this. They either followed you or were waiting in the woods for the chance. They might still be hiding on shifter land, which could be dangerous."

Since Claire had worked with politicians for nearly a decade, she'd become pretty good at sorting out lies and platitudes from truth. Her gut said Aidan was telling the truth. Although, she wondered why he believed her so easily. Maybe it had to do with his inner cougar.

Her anger eased, replaced with a small amount of nervousness. She tried to pull away, but Aidan kept his grip firm. "Let me go, Aidan. There's a lot of shit to do and not much time to do it."

"Not until I do this." He gave her a gentle kiss and released her chin. "I consider that our engagement kiss."

"Don't be silly, no such thing exists, not even in shifter culture."

"Well, there isn't exactly a handbook on engagement procedures for scandal correction and damage control."

She smiled at that. "You seem to be taking this better than I thought. I expected some stammering and pacing, to be honest. Maybe even a snarl or two."

Releasing her, he stood up and offered a hand. When she took it, he pulled her up against his body to whisper in her ear. "The way I see it, by going along with your idea, you're mine and I get to keep you."

The words sent a thrill through her body. "Well, 'keep' may be the wrong word, but I must admit I like the fact I get to keep you, too." She leaned back to look into his eyes. "My only concerns are how this might hurt the clan and Chloe."

"Let's talk to Kian first and then I'll figure out how to handle Chloe."

Sensing her shifter's worry, she touched his cheek. "You never know, Aidan, it may all work out. It doesn't have to be a complete farce. Besides, keeping the photo and our story from her will hurt her. The other kids are bound to talk tomorrow."

"I know, but Chloe has already had one mother ripped from her side. I don't want to think of her losing another."

The image of Chloe crying because of Claire leaving squeezed her heart. "Whatever happens, loving Chloe won't be a chore. She doesn't take after you in the charm department, which makes her hard to resist."

He harrumphed. "And she knows it, too. The charm comes from her mother."

Realizing this was the first time Aidan had referred to his dead mate so casually, Claire tried to keep the conversation light so as to not attract notice to it. "Well, charm or not, she's still your daughter, which means she's stubborn and stronger than you think."

"You're too clever by half, you know that, right?"

Claire grinned. "But of course."

For a second, Claire forgot about the photo and her pending fake engagement. All she saw was Aidan, tall, strong, and with mischief twinkling in his eyes.

He looked nothing like the man she first met a little less than forty-eight hours before.

His cell phone rang, breaking the spell of the moment. Picking it up off the table, Aidan answered it, "Hello?"

Claire didn't have super-sensitive hearing, so she stood not so patiently until her shifter spoke again. "We'll be there in a few."

Clicking the phone off, she raised her brows. Aidan answered, "Chloe's all squared away. The meeting with Kian is on. We need to go."

She nodded. Playfulness forgotten, Claire and Aidan made their way out the door and down the hall.

While she believed her idea of a fake engagement would work, it would mean nothing if Kian said no and kicked her off DarkStalker's land. Her future was about to be decided by a near stranger, and she hated it.

CHAPTER ELEVEN

As soon as Claire sat down across from Kian Murray, DarkStalker's leader spoke up. "Dani filled me in on what's happened and that you both know about it. She mentioned Claire possibly having a plan, but didn't know what it was. So, tell us."

Careful to keep her posture tall, Claire explained, "No amount of protesting over the photo will change anything. While you and I know nakedness is nothing to a shifter, it's not the same for humans. Me being with a naked Aidan means we're together or he's a sexual predator. I'm just glad they didn't play the sexual predator card."

Kian switched his gaze to Aidan. "What the hell were you doing naked in the first place? I'm surprised Claire agreed to follow you at all."

Aidan shrugged. "I didn't have any clothes and I needed to shift to explain things."

Kian's voice was dry. "Next time, bring a fucking bundle of clothes. Human Purity capturing that shot means they're on our lands unnoticed. We need to be more cautious from now on."

Claire jumped in. "So, you don't think I set it up myself?"

DarkStalker's leader shook his head. "No. With what's at stake with your aunt, you wouldn't jeopardize winning the vote. Shock and awe photos haven't been part of SEA's tactics, either." Kian leaned forward. "Now, tell me your plan."

The dominance in his voice urged her to follow his orders. It wasn't like she had a choice, anyway. "The photo claimed we were lovers. The best—and probably only—way to use this scandal to our advantage is to spin it as a love story. Provided, of course, you can keep the authorities from raiding DarkStalker's land and carting us away."

Sitting at Kian's side, Trinity spoke up for the first time. "When we're on high alert, keeping humans off our lands is fairly easy. Soon, not even Human Purity will stand a chance." Trinity looked to Aidan and back. "But Aidan agreed to your love story plan?"

Trinity's words stung. *Is it really such a stretch that he wants me?* Resisting the urge to kiss Aidan right then and there to show how much the shifter male desired her, she merely replied, "Yes. Why do you sound so surprised?"

Trinity smiled. "Oh, just checking. Considering how Aidan's eyes flashed when I asked the question, the story is already halfway to being true."

Before Claire could even look at Aidan, her shifter growled. "This isn't a time to tease, Trinity. Claire is mine, so leave her alone."

She felt Kian's gaze on her. Rather than chicken out, Claire met his curious gaze. After a second, Kian continued as if Trinity hadn't spoken up. "I can protect you, that's not a problem. We have a few hundred years of experience keeping the police and federal government away when we put effort into it. But before I risk my clan, I need a guarantee you can make this work. Can you?"

Claire hesitated. "I don't know. My gut says it will work, but if you want proof, I don't have any." She looked to Trinity and back. "If that's too much of a risk, then I can run and hide somewhere. I'm sure my aunt and her partner can eventually take me in."

Aidan placed a hand on her thigh and squeezed. The contact helped slow the churning in her stomach. Even if Kian said no, Aidan might find a way to help her escape and stay safe.

Of course, because of his daughter, she'd have to make sure to run away if he decided to stay with her.

Kian shared a glance with Trinity before looking back to Claire. *This was it.* "We'll protect you for a month." Aidan made a sound of protest but Kian pushed on. "If the media and press look to be leaning to our side, you can stay longer. Consider it an incentive to use every trick you have to make it a success."

Hope warmed her heart and she nodded. "I'll do whatever it takes. Thank you."

Kian raised his brows. "Oh, don't thank me just yet. In order to stay, you're going to do things my way."

Even though Claire hated not being in charge, she forced herself to say, "And what does your way entail?"

"You're going to hand over control of the Shifter Equality Alliance to your second-in-command," Kian stated.

Claire felt as if she had been kicked in the stomach. Frowning at the shifter sitting across from her, she demanded, "You want me to do what? The SEA is my baby."

Kian's face remained neutral. "Handing over the SEA to your second-in-command means you'll be off the grid and is the only way I can guarantee your safety. I also think it's the best chance at the vote still passing in November. You need to focus your energies on crafting this love story and sharing it with the press, as well as learning to defend yourself in case Human Purity tries to nab you at some point in the future. Believe me, I know how much time and effort it takes to be in charge. You won't be able to handle both."

The thought of losing control of the SEA tugged at her heart. It had been her entire life for over five years.

Giving it up would mean giving up a piece of who she was.

Aidan squeezed her thigh again under the table. Meeting his gaze, she saw support and understanding. He'd also lost a piece of himself when he'd lost his mate and unborn children.

Kian's voice broke the spell and she looked back to DarkStalker's leader. "I hate to be a bastard, but I need your answer now, Claire. Either give up the SEA and work on crafting the love story narrative, or you'll have to leave my land and deal with the backlash yourself. Each second we don't address the press is another second people will listen to the scandal and Human Purity's bullshit. We can't afford to lose many voters, but given the chance, Human Purity will spew more lies to seal the initiative's fate."

Pushing aside the feeling she was about to tear out a piece of her heart, Claire knew her best chance at surviving and helping the shifters meant sacrificing the biggest part of her life. As much as she didn't want to do it, living was more important than being in control.

She answered quietly, "I'll give up the SEA. The price of not doing so is too great."

~ ~ ~

Rubbing Claire's leg, Aidan tried to ease some of her tension. She'd just agreed to give up the center of her life. Nothing he said would help, but he would support her in any way he could. He was determined to make Claire happy again.

Rather than think about how Claire's happiness had come to mean so much to him in a short span of time, he asked Kian, "Will you allow Dani and I to plan the security for keeping Claire safe?"

Kian tapped his fingers against the table. "You can help, but I'm putting Dani in charge of this." Aidan opened his mouth but Kian cut him off. "No, you're too close to it all and your emotions will get in the way. I want you to help Claire craft her story and teach her defense moves. Once the public starts to believe the story, you'll need to make secret appearances and I want you both prepared."

Aidan frowned. "Public appearances? How in the hell can we do that? The police will have their suspicions about Claire staying with me, and they could arrest her. Living with a shifter is illegal."

Kian answered, "Did you miss the 'secret' part? With enough planning, we can get you two to speak to crowds of humans without the authorities' knowledge."

Aidan gave Kian a skeptical look. "It's still risky. I don't like it."

Claire spoke up. "Kian's right. Leaking pictures and videos will help, but without us talking with the public, there will always be rumors about it being untrue. The word-of-mouth will help us more than you can imagine."

He squeezed Claire's thigh. "Not only will it make you an easy target, secrets leak out all the time. There's no guarantee you won't be arrested."

Kian interjected, "I'm working on that. I'm going to have to ask the bears for a favor. I was putting it off, but I need to find a way to keep other humans on my land."

Claire's brows drew together. "What other humans? And the bears? What can they do?"

Aidan answered, "He's talking about Lauren, who you met the other day. Once she gives birth, she'll be here illegally."

Trinity jumped in. "As for the rest, the ShadowClaw bears are mostly lawyers. If there's any sort of loophole in the law to protect us once we step off DarkStalker's lands, they'll either know it or will find one."

Looking to Aidan, Claire asked, "Why will Lauren's status change once she has her baby? I don't understand."

Aidan answered, "Lauren is already using a loophole. Since she's carrying a half-shifter child, she has shifter DNA in her body."

Claire finished the thought, "And any person with even a trace amount of shifter DNA can choose to live with the shifters. But what about after she births the baby? What happens then if you can't find a loophole?"

Kian's voice was firm. "I'll cross that bridge when we come to it. I think we're done for now, unless you have any questions that can't wait?"

Claire shook her head. "I need to process all of this first. I'm sure we'll have another meeting soon."

Kian replied, "As soon as you hand over the SEA, we'll talk again. Not before." Since Claire didn't really have a choice, she nodded and he looked over to Aidan. "Take Claire back to her quarters." Kian looked over to Claire. "Contact your second-in-command straightaway. Once you're done, Hector will cut off your internet access. I don't want you logging on to any of your accounts."

"Without the internet or email, how am I supposed to do anything?" Claire demanded.

"You'll find a way. I'm sure others can find information for you if you request it. I will also be keeping in touch with the SEA and can pass along information." Kian stood up. "Now, I think we should all get to work. I'll touch base soon. Take the evening to settle your affairs, Claire, and then move into Aidan's apartments."

Aidan realized Kian was forgetting one important point. "What about the clan? Will they be in on the love story idea, or do we keep it secret?"

Trinity melted against Kian's side. "We'll have a claiming ceremony tomorrow evening. They'll know you're together, but not that it's a cover story. To them, it will be a whirlwind romance."

Claire looked at each person in the room. "What's a claiming ceremony? I've only heard rumors of a mating ceremony."

Trinity waved a hand at Aidan. "Aidan can explain it later. From now on, your job is to play the part of a couple madly in love. It's the only way for us to possibly have a happy ending."

Aidan's inner cougar purred at the idea of a claiming ceremony. That would be one-step closer to making Claire theirs for good.

However, his human half was a little unsure. The fact Claire was human meant he couldn't foresee the reaction of his clan. Sean Fisher mating Lauren was one thing, but their head sentry marrying a political organizer was another. Human politics had done little to help Clan DarkStalker over the years. A few of the more stubborn might take out their hatred and frustration on Claire.

He only hoped the bears could help them. There was no way in hell he would allow the human police to steal Claire away from his side. If ShadowClaw didn't have a way out, Aidan would have to dissuade both Claire and his clan leader about the public appearances.

Wrapping an arm around Claire's waist, he looked to Trinity. "Don't meddle and it will make our act easier."

Rather than wait for a reply, Aidan nodded to Kian and guided Claire out of the room.

~~~

Powering down her computer, Claire let out a sigh and covered her eyes with her forearm. Her eyes prickled, and if she wasn't careful, she would cry.

Effective immediately, she was no longer in charge of the Shifter Equality Alliance.

While she'd always figured in failure, she never in a million years expected to be forced out due to scandal. For five years, she had dedicated her life to the SEA. She could help from the outside to pass human-shifter marriage equality, but no longer could she turn tactics on their head and give orders to her team of thousands of volunteers.

While she was in shock, once everything had time to set in, she was going to need a lot of coffee and cookies to keep herself going.

Strong hands massaged her shoulders. Each rub and squeeze helped to release some tension. When Claire was sure she had her emotions mostly under control, she lowered her arms to look up into Aidan's handsome face. "Thank you."

"Well, you just had to willingly give up the most important thing in your life. That has to be worse than having it stolen from you. Either way, I more than anyone else understand a little of what you're going through."

After enjoying a few more seconds of Aidan's massage, Claire stood and turned to face him. Gently, she laid her hands on his chest and he wrapped his arms around her. Looking him in the eye, she asked, "How did you move past it? I know I'm still digesting it all, but there will soon be a giant, empty hole in my heart."

He squeezed her against him. "I had Chloe to think about. Since she was only a toddler, I went through the motions for about six months. Eventually, though, Chloe was talking and asking me why I was sad. At that point, I knew I needed to pull myself together for her."

Not wanting to pass up the rare chance, Claire risked pushing further. "How did it happen, Aidan?"

He glanced away, but she was patient. If their love story were to work, she needed to know the details of his past. Of course, she wanted to know about it for more than a cover story; Claire wanted to know everything about the man in front of her.

Aidan kept his gaze averted when he finally spoke. "Well, I guess I should start by saying shifter males are quite protective of their pregnant mates."

Claire smiled. "You don't say."

He met her gaze then, but at her smile, he smiled himself. "If you think I'm alpha now, then it would be twenty times worse if you were pregnant."

Rather than frighten her, the thought of having Aidan's child warmed her heart. Strange, considering Claire had never really thought about having children before. It must be because of Chloe. "Okay, so you were protective. Tell me the rest."

Shaking his head, Aidan continued. "Well, by Emily's sixth month of being pregnant with twins, she was stir-crazy. She wanted to shift, run, and play in the forest."

"Why couldn't she?"

"Clan leaders generally don't like pregnant females to leave the safety of the clan after about the fifth month. That's when they start to show in both their human and shifter forms. There has been a long history of poachers kidnapping pregnant shifters and keeping them until they birth the babies. Then they kill the mother and keep the cubs to train or sell into the underground slave trade."

Claire frowned. "What? Since when has there been an underground shifter slave trade?"

Aidan shrugged. "Pretty much since the beginning of time. Much like the human slave trade, it doesn't really ever get mentioned."

She was curious to know more, but didn't want to distract Aidan from his story, so she prompted, "So did Emily sneak out?"

With a sad smile, Aidan shook his head. "No, she wore me down and I agreed to take her to the safe zone, which is usually reserved for the teenagers to run around and play without fear."

Placing her arms around his waist, she gently prodded. "Tell me what happened, Aidan."

Idly, he rubbed her lower back. "While both in our cougar forms, we played chase at first, and then hunt and seek."

"Is that like hide and seek?"

"Sort of. The aim is to test our tracking skills, so the target moves around rather than stay still."

"And?"

"It was my turn to hide and evade discovery. While Emily was good and could usually find me within five minutes, fifteen minutes passed without so much as a sound. More worried than usual because of the twins, I stayed put so she could find me. After another five minutes, I knew something was wrong."

Her strong shifter male closed his eyes and took a deep breath. Even after all these years, the memories had to be painful.

Yet if she didn't hear it in this moment, then Claire wasn't sure she could truly understand Aidan. And for some reason, she wanted to understand him. Not just because of the cover story, but because she truly wanted to know everything about the strong shifter soldier who hid his pain both for the sake of his daughter as well as for his clan.

Rubbing Aidan's back in long, slow motions, she whispered, "I want to know, Aidan. Tell me."

He opened his eyes and traced her cheek. "For you, Claire, I will. I don't think I could deny you anything."

She stopped breathing at the tenderness in his voice. She was honest enough with herself to admit she was falling for him.

Afraid her voice would break, Claire nodded for him to continue and he did. "After tracking Emily, I finally found her with a bullet in the chest. Judging from the bruises and scraps of material strewn about, she had fought the poacher and lost."

Laying her head on his chest, she hugged him tightly. "I'm so sorry, Aidan."

After a few seconds of silence, he continued. "I know she's gone, but there are times when I wish she was here. Despite weighing about seventy pounds less than me, she never backed down. She wasn't afraid to call me out on my shit. She brought fire to my life in more ways than one."

Nuzzling his chest, she kept her voice strong. "I never will try to replace her. She actually sounds like someone I'd get along with. But I can certainly call you out on your shit. I think I already do."

Aidan's laugh rumbled beneath her ear and she looked up. Laughter danced in his eyes. "Yes, and don't ever stop. It's one of the things that makes me feel alive for the first time since Emily died."

Raising a hand to Aidan's cheek, she rubbed her fingers against his late-day stubble. "I can think of other things that make parts of you come alive."

His gaze turned heated. "My cock is already standing at attention. Kiss me, Claire. I think we both need something to distract us from reality." He leaned down until his lips nearly touched hers. "Besides, I think we need to practice our loving couple façade. Fucking you hard will definitely have you fawning over me later."

Heat rushed through her body, making her wet. Aidan could probably scent her, but she was going to make him work for it. "I don't know about that. It's going to take some rather spectacular sex to make me fawn over anyone."

Growling, Aidan drew her closer against his body. "You won't fawn over any other male. Just me."

She raised an eyebrow. "Oh, is that so? Then you better start convincing me."

Without another word, he kissed her.

Chapter Twelve

Telling Claire about Emily's death lifted some of the weight off Aidan's shoulders. Sure, Dani and Kian knew the truth of what had happened, but this was the first time he had ever willingly shared the experience with someone.

Not only that, Claire didn't dismiss Emily or show any jealously over his former mate. He believed her when she said she wouldn't try to replace Emily. With time, Aidan might be able to share some of his happier memories with both Claire and Chloe. Chloe always asked about her mother. If Claire remained at his side, he could probably tell Chloe whatever she needed, even treasuring the good times.

Then his human teased about bringing other parts of him to life and another neglected part of his anatomy had spoken. Twice with Claire earlier hadn't been enough for his cock. Hell, a million times probably wouldn't be enough.

So he kissed her. Since the door was locked against any intruders, Aidan ran his hands under Claire's top and grabbed one of her breasts. Pinching her nipple, the smell of her arousal grew stronger as she moaned into his mouth.

The sound made his cougar purr and demand more, much more.

Aidan agreed, and with a growl, he broke the kiss. "Foreplay can happen later. Right now, I want you naked and on your hands and knees on our bed."

Desire flashed in her eyes, but there was also amusement. "Playing the part of a 'loving couple' doesn't mean I do whatever you say."

Maneuvering his hands, he took Claire's wrists. "Just this once, I think you will." Nuzzling her neck, he bit her gently and she sucked in a breath. "Why, you wonder?" He nibbled some more. "Because I bet you've been thinking about the 'shifter way'." He raised a knee and pressed it between her legs. Claire gasped as he rubbed her clit through her jeans and he continued, "If you want it, then undress and do as I asked."

Pressing a little harder, Claire leaned into his touch before whispering, "You're teasing me on purpose, you bastard."

Chuckling, he rubbed his cheek against hers and lowered his leg. "Well, we do have a lot of planning to do. I can easily let you go and teach you self-defense moves instead."

After a beat of silence, Claire answered, "I should, so that I can evade you next time."

"Ah, but do you really want to evade me?"

He bit her earlobe and blew on her wet flesh. His cougar was all but snarling inside his head to fuck their human, but Aidan kept his cat in check. They were going to do this Aidan's way.

Claire finally grunted. "Fine, but next time, you'll have to catch me first."

The thought of chasing their human in the forest before taking her under the stars gave Aidan and his cougar all kinds of ideas. She may be human, but they could still play chase. "Deal. Now, strip and bare that gorgeous body for me."

He nearly added, "And only for me. Mine," but decided against it. He didn't want to argue; he wanted to fuck.

Releasing Claire, she turned and exaggerated the sway of her hips. Reveling in the sight of her full, plump ass, he nearly rushed over and ripped off her clothes. But Claire's husky voice stopped him. "Aren't you going to come watch?"

She disappeared into his bedroom. Unbuttoning his fly on the way, Aidan took his dick in hand and stroked. Watching Claire strip was going to be the ultimate test of his self-control, but one he would rather enjoy.

~ ~ ~

Claire tried her best not to blush. She had no experience stripping for men. Why she'd taunted Aidan, she didn't know.

Yet as she stopped in front of the bed and Aidan entered with his cock in his hand and heat in his eyes, a thrill twined through her body. She had never felt so desired in her life.

So don't fuck it up. Okay, but where to start?

Aidan shucked his jeans and boxers. Her eyes zeroed in on his cock and she resisted licking her lips. One day, she was going to lick him slowly until he clutched the sheets and begged her to suck him hard. Yes, one day she would be the one with the power, teasing him.

She nearly started at that thought. Making plans for the future was risky. Who the hell knew what would happen a week from this moment.

Aidan growled, "I'm waiting, but not for much longer. I will rip off your clothes, Claire."

Instead of sticking out her tongue, Claire decided to start. If he wanted to play dirty, she would play dirty.

Cupping her breasts over her sweater, she squeezed them as she leaned back her head. Closing her eyes, she pretended it was Aidan touching her as she pinched and rolled her nipples. The slight pain mixed with pleasure only made her wetter, so she pinched harder and let out a moan.

"Holy fuck," Aidan whispered.

Smiling, she opened her eyes and moved her hands to the hem of her top. Inch-by-inch, she revealed her skin, until her breasts, enclosed in a simple cotton bra, were exposed. Quickly, she tugged her sweater off and scooped out her breasts. They were still high because of the underwire, but they would draw Aidan's eye.

She placed one bare foot on the bed and leaned over to run her hand up her calf, then her knee, and then her thigh. Peeking at Aidan, she moved her hand to the seam of her jeans and pressed against her clit. She was tempted to rub some more, but resisted. She wanted to orgasm with Aidan, not alone.

Aidan took a step toward her and she raised an eyebrow. "I'm not done yet."

His voice was hoarse, not to mention his eyes glowed amber. "Claire, baby, with your boobs out and you rubbing your clit, I don't know how much longer I can hold back. My cougar is close to taking over."

She gave what she hoped was a sexy smile. "But I'm having so much fun."

He took another step closer. "Later, my human, you can tease me later. If I'm not inside you in the next minute, I'm going to explode."

"In more ways than one?"

Groaning, he squeezed the head of his cock. "When my animal is this close, innuendos only make things worse."

Noticing the cords of his neck, no doubt straining against the urge to toss her to the bed and rip her clothes off, Claire unzipped her jeans. "You had better make this worth it, Aidan Scott."

His eyes latched onto her pointed nipples. "I intend to make it worth it at least three times."

Shucking her jeans, and then her panties, she stood naked but for the bra holding up her boobs. "Four."

With a voice deeper than normal, he growled, "Fine. Now take off the damn bra and get on all fours on the bed. You have thirty seconds."

Normally, she would challenge him to draw it out. But between his gravelly voice and glowing amber eyes, she didn't want to taunt his cougar. Despite working so long for shifter rights, she knew little about what happened when you pushed a shifter's animal-side too far when it came to sex.

Quickly, she slipped off her bra straps and unhooked it. Just as she kneeled on the bed, on her hands and knees, she felt Aidan's hands caressing her ass. Any doubts she'd had about him wanting her, ass dimples and all, vanished. Each stroke of his hand warmed her skin.

She had expected him to thrust his cock into her pussy and piston away. Yet after petting her butt, he ran his hands along her back and around to just below her breasts. His hands were close enough she could feel the heat of his body, but he didn't touch her.

Widening her legs, she arched her back, but the bastard moved his hands away. Looking over her shoulder, she narrowed her eyes. "What happened to 'I'm going to lose control'? You seem pretty fucking in control right now."

His eyes flashed as a smile touched his lips. "That's because I have you naked and at my mercy."

"So you made up the 'shifter way' just to get me on all fours?"

Leaning down, his breath was a hot whisper on her lower back. "This is just part of it. With you spread wide for me and my cougar, wet and ready for my dick, my cat is content to play a little. I need to make sure you're ready, because I plan to fuck you hard."

With Aidan behind her, mentioning wanting to fuck her hard, she was close to dripping down her leg. "I'm ready and more than curious."

Running his hands up her back to her shoulders, he leaned against her ass. On instinct, she wiggled against him. At his hiss, she smiled. "That is minor compared to what I plan to do to you later."

One of his hands left her shoulder. "I look forward to it, my little human." He cupped her right breast, loving the roughness of his palms. "Because, after all, you're mine."

Before she digested his words, let alone responded to them, he positioned his cock and thrust into her.

~~~

Inside Claire's tight, wet pussy, Aidan nearly came right then.

The vixen wiggled her hips and clenched his cock. With a hiss, he grabbed her hips and ordered, "Stay still or I pull out."

Her glare was meant to threaten, but the way her eyes flashed as her brown hair tumbled over her shoulder only made him want to claim her all the more. "Then hurry up. I'm ready."

Smiling, he ran one of his hands across her back. He loved the warmth of her skin.

Massaging her full hip with his other hand, he loved how soft she was. Most shifters were all muscle and long limbs. Claire might be short and plump, but fuck; he wouldn't change a single thing about her body.

Well, except maybe one day she would grow rounder when she carried his child.

His hand stilled at that thought, but at his cougar's urging, he pushed it away. The cat was tired of waiting. They needed to fuck the human. Aidan was more than willing to comply.

Taking hold of her hips again, he pulled almost all the way out and then thrust in hard, his balls slapping against Claire's skin. He ordered, "Lean down on your forearms so I can fuck you deeper."

For once, she complied, or mostly so. Claire wiggled her hips as she adjusted her position, clenching as she did so.

He murmured, "Payback is a bitch," before pulling out and pounding in.

Claire squeaked and he repeated his movement, increasing his speed with each thrust. Claire's breasts moved in time with him, her squeaks slowly growing into moans.

Ah, but this is just the beginning. Lifting her hips higher, he changed the angle and Claire screamed his name, making his inner cougar purr.

Yet his cat wasn't nearly finished. The shifter way meant owning her pussy until she begged.

Flesh slapping against flesh filled the room, and soon sweat trailed down Aidan's back. It was taking every ounce of control he had not to come inside Claire. Unlike most human males, shifters always took care of their females. Satisfied females would never want to leave.

Claire whispered, "Please, Aidan, I'm so close."

He smiled. Outside of the bedroom, Claire would never ask him for something in a voice so close to begging.

Since his female had done well, he moved one hand and brushed her clit, eliciting a, "Yes, harder," from her.

So, of course, Aidan kept his touch gentle as he teased her tight bud. He'd stroked, paused, and then ran his thumb back and forth. The way Claire arched into his touch made him smile.

He looked forward to teasing her a lot more in the future.

His cougar growled and said it was time. She wouldn't forget their cock any time soon. They could play more later.

Pressing harder against her clit, he rubbed in circles as he thrust. Claire clenched her hands in the sheets and screamed as she came hard, gripping and releasing his cock. The tightness of her pussy was too much, and he pulled out before he came.

Claire demanded, "What the hell, Aidan?"

Gripping the head of his cock and squeezing, he willed his dick to behave. "That was just the warm-up round. You need to come again before I do."

Some of the irritation eased from her eyes. "Does this mean listening to you again?"

He grinned. "Oh, yes, my human. If you want another orgasm, lay on your side."

For a second, he didn't think she'd obey. Then Claire lay on the bed and muttered, "This had better be fucking worth it."

Chuckling, Aidan released his cock and ran a hand up the back of her thigh, her buttocks, and then her back. "Your skin is so soft."

"While I appreciate the compliment, I'm getting cold."

His cat urged him to fuck her again. Keeping a female waiting wasn't good. She might leave.

He brushed the back of her knees before lifting her leg up. Using his free hand, he lightly traced the lips of her swollen pussy. "Let's make sure you're wet enough."

Raising her leg higher, he thrust two fingers into her pussy and began to finger her. At Claire's moan, he smiled. "I think you're ready."

"I'm going to repeat that payback will be a bitch the next chance I get."

Swirling inside her, Claire moved against his fingers. "If that's supposed to deter me, it has the opposite effect. Just thinking of your plump lips around my cock makes my balls draw up tightly in anticipation."

Moving position, Claire nearly screamed. Good. He'd enter at that angle.

He removed his fingers and straddled Claire's bottom leg. Positioning his cock, he murmured, "Now this is the shifter way."

Entering hard, she moaned his name. With a cocky smile, he rocked his hips, careful to hit the spot that drove his female crazy.

As he increased his pace, it became harder and harder not to come. The tightness of her pussy at this angle was fucking incredible.

Claire twisted her hands in the sheets. "Touch me, Aidan. I'm so close it hurts."

"Begging twice in less than twenty minutes. I like it."

She started to growl but as he swirled his hips, it turned into a moan. She finally answered, "Fine, I'll beg. Just make me come. Please."

With his cat pressuring him to obey, Aidan slapped her ass cheek once before running a hand over her hip. Leaning slightly to extend his reach, he nuzzled her leg next to his face, kissed it gently, and then brushed her clit and then again.

"Mm, yes. Harder."

Pressing against her nub, Claire arched her back as she screamed his name.

Aidan didn't stop moving, loving the feel of her spasming around his dick.

As Claire came down from her orgasm, he let go of his control, slamming into her pussy before pulling back and repeating the process all over again.

The pressure was building at the base of his spine and his cat wanted to brand her.

Between the wet heat of Claire's pussy, her scent, and feel of her soft skin against his, Aidan agreed with his cougar and finally let go. Roaring her name, he stilled and filled her with his seed.

His cougar was smug. She would carry his scent for hours, at least.

After his cock gave one final spasm, he leaned over Claire's body and kissed her damp shoulder. "Holy hell, woman, you nearly killed me."

A chuckled rumbled under his lips before she answered, "Glad you think that way, because I rather thought it was the other way around."

"So I take it by your screams you like the shifter way."

Claire battled a smile. "Maybe, but if you expect me to beg every night, you're in for a surprise."

"Hell, I'll settle for every other night."

His female shook her head. "Men."

Pulling out, he moved up and rolled Claire on top of him. "Hey, you could always do your payback later. I won't complain."

Shaking her head again, Claire snuggled into his chest and he held her close in silence. The quiet wasn't strained, though, but rather comfortable. He could only imagine what was running through her mind.

Breathing in her scent as he kissed her hair, both man and cat were content in a way Aidan hadn't believed he could be again. A soft, warm female with spirit had dropped into his life and made him feel again. Not only that, she was intelligent and Chloe adored her.

Claire was his second chance.

His human may not know it yet, but whatever it took, he wasn't letting her go. Fuck the authorities and their bullshit laws. He was keeping her.

CHAPTER THIRTEEN

Listening to Aidan's heartbeat, Claire's brain slowly started working again. While sore, she would love to go a few more rounds until Aidan reached his promised four orgasms. Yet she couldn't help feeling a little guilty.

Here she was enjoying the clever and playful shifter at her side while his daughter had no idea how her life would soon change forever.

Rubbing her hand through Aidan's light spattering of chest hair, she sighed. "As much as I want to spend the rest of the day with you, we need to get our story straight and talk to Chloe. I'll take a rain check on the other orgasms you owe me."

Aidan stroked her hip in silence. Just as Claire was about to speak up again, his voice rumbled inside his chest, "I love that you think of my daughter over your own needs. You're a special kind of woman, Claire Davis."

Lifting her head, she looked up into his eyes. "Considering you agreed to play the part of my fiancé, I would say you're a special kind of man."

He squeezed her hip. "Oh, I'm not going to be playing the part. You're mine, Claire. I'm keeping you."

She waited for panic or outrage, but nothing came. If anything, her heart skipped a beat in agreement. Choosing her words carefully, she asked, "It's only been a couple days. How can you be sure?"

Hooking a finger under her chin, his eyes flashed amber. "Because you're smart, sexy, and don't put up with my shit. I also feel lighter than I have since Emily's death. Not only that, I've seen how you act with Chloe. You treat her as your own daughter, and I can see Chloe likes you. All of that in one package is pretty rare. Why the hell would I give it up?" He moved his thumb to her lower lip. "Outside forces might have pushed us together, but being assigned to retrieve you was the best fucking thing that has happened to me in a long while. Give me a chance, Claire, and I will treat you like the queen you are." He pulled her lower lip and released. "Or, rather, should I say president? You are rather used to being in charge."

Claire finally let out the breath she'd been holding and smiled. "I'm glad you realize that now, because I'm not ever going to be some weak, doormat of a woman. I'm always going to keep you on your toes, Aidan Scott, if you'll have me."

Aidan lifted her chin a fraction and searched her eyes. Claire wasn't sure where the words had come from considering it'd been two days, but everything just felt right with Aidan in a way she'd never felt before. Hell, the one man she'd been with for a year hadn't synced with Claire as much as Aidan had in the past two days.

She may be thirty-one years old, but as she waited for Aidan's reply, her heart beat overtime as if she were a teenage girl asking a boy out on a date. It hadn't been done often in her time, and the result could be unpredictable.

Then Aidan grinned and relief flooded her body. "You do realize what this means, then?"

Okay, that wasn't the response she expected. "What?"

Aidan leaned down until his face was mere inches from hers. "That we're going to fight for marriage equality for real."

She blinked. *Marriage.* The word didn't scare her. Rather, it made their success all the more critical. "If that is a proposal, Aidan Scott, then you need to up your game."

Laughing, Aidan scooted back and pulled Claire upright until she was sitting at his side. Cupping her cheek, he cleared his throat. "Well, seeing as it's illegal for now, asking seems unnecessary."

She glared. "Insufferable shifter."

He winked. "Yep, and you're stuck with me, my little human because I won't take no for an answer."

Rolling her eyes, she sighed. "I can see you're not going to make this easy on me."

"No." He drew her onto his lap and wrapped his arms around her waist. "But you wouldn't want it any other way."

Battling a grin, she lost. "Will you do all the cooking, at least?"

"Oh, I think I could manage that." He leaned in until his lips were a hair's breadth from hers. "Kiss me to seal the deal, then."

Placing a gentle kiss on his lips, she pulled away. Aidan growled, but Claire shook her head. "No more for now. We need to get our facts straight for the clan and then talk to Chloe."

Squeezing her close, Aidan murmured, "The facts are pretty simple. You prodded and pushed until I couldn't help but notice you."

"Okay, that makes me sound desperate, like I wanted to trap you or something."

Grinning, he caressed her cheek. "Other shifters will understand, so you'll have to think of the human way to explain things."

"Well, most human females will see your face and think I went after you because of your hotness."

He frowned. "Hotness? At thirty-nine, I'm nearly ancient by human media standards."

Claire bit his lip. It was cute the way Aidan doubted his sexiness. To be honest, once they were in public, Claire was going to have her hands full keeping other women away. "They say forty is the new thirty." She winked. "You're in your prime, which I can very much attest to if asked."

With a grunt, he replied, "Fine. But getting back to the story, I think the truth is best. You may not realize it, but you're irresistible, Claire, and any man who doesn't realize that is a fool."

Aidan's eyes were honest and it warmed her heart. He was definitely a keeper. "Look at you being all romantic. It's a far cry from the verbally stunted shifter who walked naked with me in the snow."

"Like you can complain. I saw you check out my cock more than once."

Claire's cheeks heated. "Yes, well, it was hard to miss."

He grinned. "Was it, now?" Her cheeks grew even hotter at being called out. Aidan laughed and kissed her nose. "As much as I love seeing you shy and embarrassed for a change, we should probably clean up and talk with Chloe. I want her to hear the information from us and not through the grapevine."

"I agree, and not just because it will stop you from teasing me some more."

After giving Claire a quick, rough kiss, he slid her off his lap. "Oh, I will be doing a lot more teasing. You haven't seen anything yet."

Crawling off the bed, she stood and looked down at him. "Good, because that means war and I intend to win."

With a growl, he reached for her but Claire moved out of the way and rushed to the bathroom door. She paused long enough to say, "Showering together will distract you, so you can shower at your place. I'll come over when I'm done, after you've left."

He strode toward the door, but she shut and locked it. At his growl, she giggled. Yes, being with Aidan Scott would never be dull.

~~~

Aidan walked home to his apartment, hand-in-hand with his daughter. Her silence worried him, but Aidan's brother had assured him that Chloe didn't know about the photo.

Yet glancing down at his daughter, her inner cat must sense the tension in the clan. Just because Chloe didn't know about the leaked photo didn't mean everyone else was ignorant, too.

Squeezing Chloe's hand, he wanted to make her smile. "Did you want left over enchiladas for dinner? I know how you love them reheated."

Chloe shook her head, her mop of tight curls bouncing. "No, there's not enough for everyone. Claire's coming to dinner, isn't she? It would be mean to eat them in front of her."

The corner of his mouth ticked up. "Yes, Claire will be eating dinner with us. Do you have any recommendations? Since you survived my 'learning to cook' phase, you know better than anyone what to avoid. I don't want to make her sick."

Chloe smiled up at him. "Then don't make stew. The meat always turns out weird and the carrots too mushy."

"Okay, no stew. How about chow mein?"

At the mention of her second favorite food, Chloe's eyes lit up. "Yes, we should definitely have chow mein." Her look grew suspicious. "You never make enchiladas and chow mein back-to-back. You say it will spoil me and everyone should learn to eat things they don't like very much."

Damn. His daughter was too smart for her own good.

As they made the final turn to their apartment, he picked up his pace. "Well, I can make curry, if you like."

Chloe scrunched up her nose. "That is another food you shouldn't make Claire. You always make it too spicy."

Arriving at the door, he nodded as he turned the knob. "I'll keep that in mind."

Claire was sitting on the sofa, her hair still damp from the shower. She wore his baggy sweatshirt and a pair of yoga pants, no doubt to taunt him with the shape of her legs.

Thankfully, Chloe raced over to Claire before he could think too much about his human's legs and Chloe clapped her hands. "Guess what Daddy's making for dinner?"

Claire sat up straighter with a smile. "Something good, I hope."

Chloe nodded. "Yes, chow mein. It's another specialty. I think he wants to spoil you so you'll stay." Chloe glanced over her shoulder at her dad and then back to whisper, "But I hope it works. I like you Claire. Daddy smiles more when you're around."

Aidan watched as Claire's face softened. Then his human tucked some curls behind Chloe's ear. "So you want me to stay, then, if I could?"

Chloe nodded. "Yes, but Lauren says it's difficult for humans to live here. Only because she stays all the time can our clan protect her." His daughter sat on the edge of the sofa and touched Claire's hair. "Are you going to stay all the time? Daddy would be happy and you would make a good mommy."

Aidan held his breath. Chloe was always bold with words, but he could hear the thread of longing in her voice.

Claire framed Chloe's face with her hands. "I would like it very much, but only if you don't mind. I would be living with you and your daddy and I don't want to ruin things. After all, you two have been a team for a long time before I came."

Without hesitation, Chloe answered, "Yes, but our team has room for more. You should stay. Then you can help me with my paper flowers. I want to learn how to make a really good one by myself that isn't all crumpled."

Aidan wished he could leave it at that, but he needed to make sure his daughter fully understood the situation. He walked over to her and crouched until he was eye level. Staring into his daughter's amber eyes, he kept his voice cautious. "Chloe, love, if Claire stays, she'll be my mate."

His daughter bobbed her head. "I like that. Then maybe I can have a little brother or sister. I've always wanted one. Then I'd have someone to play with all the time."

Aidan blinked. "What?"

Chloe shrugged. "You can't have a baby by yourself. You need a female."

Aidan cleared his throat. "Claire might not have any children. Is that the only reason you want her to stay?"

Chloe glanced to Claire and back to him. "No, you also act different around Claire. You laugh and smile. Jeff's parents always laugh and smile together, so I hoped Claire would stay. I don't like you sad, Daddy."

His throat closed with emotion as he pulled his daughter into a hug. After kissing her hair, he whispered, "You're the best daughter in the world, Chloe Nicole Scott. I love you."

"I love you too, Daddy." Chloe leaned back and there was mischief in her eyes. "Maybe tomorrow you can cook me lasagna as a reward."

Laughing, he looked to Claire and explained, "Lasagna is her third favorite food. She's determined to go down the list."

Claire smiled and then winked at Chloe. "Well, your daddy has agreed to cook every day, so you can help me plan the dinners."

He sighed. "It's going to be two against one from now on, isn't it?"

Chloe patted his shoulder. "Don't worry. I will sometimes be on your side, just so you don't get lonely."

As everyone laughed, Aidan moved until he could hug Chloe with one arm and Claire with the other. Through a strange web of events, he finally had a family again and he would do whatever it took to protect them. There was no way in hell he was going to lose them if he could help it.

Chapter Fourteen

The next evening, Aidan guided Claire and Chloe into the main meeting area. While Claire knew it was usually used for announcements and clan gatherings, she hadn't expected a large cavern full of stalactites glowing with soft lighting. Or, to find a large stage decorated in evergreen boughs, ribbon, and gold and silver draping material.

Aidan nodded toward the stage. "That's for us, Claire."

While she was determined to stay with Aidan, seeing the stage made everything seem more real and her stomach flipped.

Everything will be fine. Sure, she had no idea what to expect living with DarkStalker long term, but Aidan, Kian, and even little Chloe would help her through it all.

Pushing aside her nervousness, she replied, "It's beautiful. Although, if those decorations are just for a claiming ceremony, I can't imagine what they would be for a mating ceremony."

Chloe spoke up. "It's much simpler. But I hope you don't mind blood. The cutting palms and holding hands part is a little gross."

Claire had researched shifter mating ceremonies as part of her job. After all, the problem was human law not recognizing the matings as a legal marriage, which in the case of human-shifter pairings, should grant certain privileges. She only hoped when her time came, she could cut her palm without flinching.

Provided, of course, she wasn't arrested first.

Rather than think about the work she and Aidan had to do before November, she focused on the empty space. "Where is everyone, by the way? It's really empty with just us."

Aidan motioned toward the stage with his head. "We'll stand up there, and then everyone will be allowed in. The point of the claiming ceremony is to show the entire clan that you belong to me."

As they approached the stage, she raised an eyebrow. "So, I'm property then? Are you going to sell me if I don't behave?"

Chloe giggled. "No, silly. Daddy can't sell you. He belongs to you too. Shifter mates belong to each other."

Her soon-to-be stepdaughter's giggles were infectious and Claire couldn't help but smile. "Well, that I can live with. Although, your daddy belongs to more than just me. He belongs to both of us."

Chloe nodded. "Yes, so we need to protect him."

Aidan rolled his eyes. "I'm standing right here. Did you conveniently forget that I'm one of the head sentries? I can protect myself."

Chloe beat her to the punch. "Our job is to protect you from sadness."

They ascended the few steps to the stage and Aidan moved them both in front of him before releasing their hands. "Somehow, I don't think it's sadness I'll need protecting from."

Grinning, Claire tilted her head. "What, are you afraid of little old us?"

He grunted. "The two of you together will bring trouble."

Claire was about to tease her man further when the giant wooden doors at the far side of the cavern opened. Kian and Trinity slipped in and then the door closed behind them.

Immediately, the playfulness and ease disappeared. Even Chloe straightened her shoulders as Kian approached, his limp in no way diminishing the control and dominance he exuded. Being steady all the time for the sake of the clan had to be exhausting.

For the first time, it hit Claire how lonely being clan leader could be.

Then Trinity wrapped an arm around Kian's waist and Claire realized DarkStalker's leader would always have his mate to lean upon.

Kian smiled and nodded at each of them in turn. "Everyone's waiting, if you're prepared."

Aidan looked to Claire. "Ready to go?" When she nodded, he looked to Chloe. "And how about you?"

Chloe raised her chin. "I'm ready, Daddy."

Kian smiled. "Good. Then let's get started."

As he pulled out his cell phone and texted a message, Trinity moved closer to the stage. "Come, Chloe. We can watch from the front row."

Claire took a step toward Trinity. "Can't she stay? She's claiming me as much as Aidan."

Approval flashed in Trinity's eyes. "That's the right answer. I think you're going to do just fine here, Claire Davis." Trinity looked to Chloe. "As long as you promise to behave, you can stay on stage. Can you do that?" After Chloe bobbed her head, Trinity looked to Aidan and Claire. "All right, it's show time."

Aidan drew Claire to his side and whispered into her ear, "Just act with them like you act around me and you'll do fine."

"Not everyone approves of humans intermingling, let alone mating with the shifters."

He shrugged. "Too bad. Once Kian endorses the claim in front of the clan, they'll have little choice but to accept you. If they're really against it, they can always leave. After all, Lauren is part of the clan; they need to accept the both of you."

Some shifters did leave their clans to become loners, although it was rare. Still, some of those loners had been invaluable in her campaign get as far as it had.

Well, her former campaign. The fact she was no longer in charge still stung.

Sensing her unease, Aidan squeezed her side. His gaze was full of confidence and even a little tenderness.

Not wanting to disappoint her man, Claire straightened her shoulders and whispered, "Bring it on."

Aidan smiled before the doors opened and everyone filed in.

~~~

As soon as his clan filed in, Aidan went on high alert. His cat was anxious to spot any threats to either their new mate or their daughter.

Hey, she's not our mate yet.

His cat didn't agree. Even without a ceremony, she was theirs.

Hoping his cougar would channel that possessiveness into something useful, Aidan scanned the room. Dani entered first, followed by some of Aidan's soldiers. Next came his brother, his brother's mate, and some of his friends. His allies would stand near the front of the room, as a type of buffer and visible reminder of support to those who might oppose the match.

But as the cavern filled up, Aidan finally spotted some of the anti-human minded shifters. Most of them were older and were used to shifter and human segregation, believing it was the reason they had stayed safe over the years.

The only good news was that they stood at the very back of the room. There were close to two hundred shifters in the room, and even if the anti-human faction managed to shift, his soldiers and friends would stop any threats before they reached the stage. Of course, even if they managed to get past Dani, they still had to deal with Aidan.

Once the giant doors were closed, Kian took the steps on the side of the stage slowly, one at a time, and limped his way to the middle. Putting up his hands, Kian spoke once there was silence. "This evening, we celebrate our own Aidan Scott. It is rare to find a second chance, but he has done so in Claire Davis. As both leader and friend to Aidan, I fully support his choice of future mate. Any who oppose the match may talk with me privately. However, barring any concrete proof as to why this match shouldn't go forward, we should have another mating before long."

Aidan watched the back of the crowd. A few of the shifters were whispering with each other, but so far, no one had dared to challenge Kian openly.

Claire squeezed his waist and he looked down at his beautiful human. Strength and determination glinted in her eyes, which only strengthened his resolve to do the claiming properly.

Kian's voice filled the cavern again. "Come forward, Aidan Scott, and make your claim."

Normally, Aidan wasn't one for public speaking. Dani handled that aspect of their shared duties much better than he. Yet as Kian motioned for him to come forward, he mustered all of his stubbornness and protectiveness, giving him the strength to speak loudly and clearly when he reached the front of the stage.

"Claire Davis is my choice and I claim her. With my claim, she has the protection of me, our leader, and the clan as a whole. To harm her would be to harm one of DarkStalker."

A few murmurs rose up from the back of the room, but Aidan ignored them and faced Claire. "With the clan as our witness, do you accept my claim?"

Claire's voice was strong when she answered, "Yes, I do."

Cupping the cheek of his brave little human, he gave her a gentle kiss. Applause rose and Aidan decided what the hell, and kissed her again. However, this time, he slipped his tongue into her mouth and pulled her tight against his body.

When he finished, Claire's face was flushed and she was out of breath. She whispered, "At least you didn't try to rip my clothes off. That's a relief."

He murmured his reply, "I was tempted, but then too many males would see your body."

She smiled at that, but before she could say anything else, Kian touched their shoulders. "The claim is complete and has been witnessed. Those who have a complaint can come speak with me privately. Today is a time to celebrate, not to cause an unnecessary rift in the clan." Kian looked over the crowd slowly, lingering on the old-timers at the back. While they didn't look happy, they weren't about to challenge Kian. At least, not this evening; no doubt, they would think of a plan eventually. Kian nodded. "Now that's out of the way, how about some music to celebrate?"

As cheers went up from most of the crowd, upbeat music filled the cavern and Kian turned toward Aidan and Claire. "As much as I'm sure you want to rip each other's clothes off and enjoy a wild night of sex, I need you to mingle. The purpose of this event is for the clan to get to know Claire. The more the clan thinks of you as their own, the less we'll have to worry about the older clan members causing trouble."

Aidan asked, "Have you heard anything specific?"

"No," Kian answered. "But while they grudgingly accepted Lauren, they might see Claire's addition as a trend that needs to be stopped. However, I'm a few steps ahead and have a few spies among them. The second there's talk of serious trouble, I'll know."

Aidan nodded. "Good. Let me know if I can help."

Kian slapped him on the shoulder. "I will, but not tonight. You two should go have some fun."

Claire spoke up. "But what about Chloe? We can't leave her alone and I don't want her to accidentally hear rude comments thrown our way. Just because there won't be major trouble doesn't mean people won't be assholes to me."

Aidan looked at his daughter, who was chatting with Trinity. "Maybe Trin could watch her? After all, she needs the practice."

Kian frowned. "You aren't supposed to know that yet."

Aidan shrugged. "Dani noticed first. Besides, it's our job to protect your future young."

Claire glanced to Trinity and back to Aidan. "She's pregnant? She can't be far along since she's still quite thin."

Kian's voice was dry. "She prefers athletic, although her pregnancy hormones have convinced her she's already fat."

Aidan winked at his clan leader. "Good luck with that one, Kian. It'll only get worse, especially considering you're a twin and Trinity might be pregnant with twins herself."

Kian sighed. "Don't remind me." He scanned the crowd. "Speaking of which, Sylas should be around here somewhere with Kaya. I told Dani to let them in after the claiming."

Aidan spotted Sy in the crowd. "I see them." He looked back to his clan leader. "You can help Trinity with Chloe. You'll need the practice as well because there's no way in hell Trin will allow you to back away from baby duty."

"Fine," Kian said. "Enjoy yourselves because from tomorrow, your schedules will be a mixture of clan duties, training, and strategy sessions with me and Kaya about how to use your pairing to win the vote in November without getting arrested."

Nodding at his clan leader, he pressed gently against Claire's back. "Come, Claire. It's time for you to charm the rest of the clan."

She looked at him with amusement. "Let's just hope none of them try to 'charm' me by shucking their clothes to shift. It'll be hard not to look, and then you'll probably punch them in the face." She tapped her chin and continued before Aidan could do anything but blink. "Come to think of it, I want to see more cougar-shifters in their cat forms and hear them purr. Maybe I should ask them since you don't do it enough."

He growled, which made Claire laugh. As he guided her down the stairs of the stage, he murmured, "I can shift and purr for you later. For now, just promise me you won't ask everyone to shift so you can pet them."

Her eyes were bright with mirth. "I'll try not to."

Squeezing her tightly against his side, Aidan readied himself for the crowd.

~~~

With a smile on her face, Claire studied the crowd as Aidan guided her to a man he said was his brother. While younger, the other shifter male had the same brown eyes and dark hair. The woman leaning against his side had to be his mate, and like most non-middle-aged shifters, she was tall and athletic with perceptive, assessing eyes.

Still, the woman smiled, her white teeth bright against her dark skin. When they were only a few feet away, Aidan nodded. "Jeremy, Naomi, this is Claire."

Naomi spoke up first. "We've heard a lot about you from Chloe. It's nice to meet you."

The woman's words rang genuine, so Claire extended a hand. "I know Aidan's grateful for you helping out with Chloe, so I am too."

The younger version of Aidan, Jeremy, took her hand. "Any female who can put up with my brother's stubborn ass deserves a gold medal. Anytime you need an escape, you can come over for a while."

Aidan grunted and everyone laughed. When Claire finally caught her breath, she replied, "I'll keep that in mind, although my stubbornness rivals his, so he may be fleeing to you."

While it was said in jest, Claire had experienced a man or two who hadn't liked a strong, determined woman. As a young woman in her twenties, she questioned if she should remain stubborn or give in more often.

Then Aidan squeezed her tighter against him, and she was grateful for never giving up. Standing toe-to-toe with Aidan was more fun than she could ever remember.

Naomi's voice interrupted Claire's thoughts. "Well, you can't just keep Claire all to yourself, Aidan. Bring her around for dinner soon, with Chloe, of course, so we can tell her all the good stories."

Claire raised her brows. "Oh, I'd like to hear the good stories. I hope they're extra embarrassing."

Naomi laughed. "Some of them are, although we may have to wait until Aidan is out the room before I share."

Aidan frowned and jumped in. "We'll talk about you violating my privacy later, Naomi. Right now, I need to show Claire off."

Jeremy's face grew serious. "Just be careful, brother. There's talk in the clan about her ruining our image because of the leaked photo."

Claire's brows drew together. "How could I ruin the clan's image?"

Jeremy answered, "Some think it was planned. Or, if Aidan had never had to meet with you, we could have kept the humans away. The fear is that the media attention will bring reckless shifter groupies and poachers. The latter worries me."

Aidan gripped his brother's shoulder. "Don't worry, brother, we'll be careful. First thing tomorrow, I'll talk with Dani about extra patrols and surveillance, if she hasn't implemented them already herself."

"I don't doubt you, Aidan," Jeremy stated.

Aidan released his brother's shoulder. "Good. For now, I see Sylas in the crowd and I need to talk with him. I'll touch base with you tomorrow."

After saying their goodbyes, Aidan guided Claire back into the crowd. She noticed that the further they went from the stage, the less friendly the smiles.

Then a man who looked remarkably like Kian Murray appeared in front of them with the leader of the GreyFire wolves at his side. With a grin, Kian's twin winked. "All the gorgeous humans showed up after I left. Makes me wonder if I did the right thing."

Kaya punched him and he faked being hurt. "That may never get old for you, but it's getting a little old for me. You touch another female and I'll cut off your dick in your sleep, Sylas Murray."

Claire blinked. But then Sylas leaned down to whisper something into Kaya's ear, which she couldn't hear, and the corner of Kaya's mouth ticked up. Claire was tempted to ask what he'd whispered, but then Aidan spoke up. "Stop flirting with my human, Sylas, or I'll cut off your balls in your sleep."

Sylas gave an exaggerated look of offense. "I was just trying to give a compliment."

Aidan grunted. "Sometimes, I'm glad you left. Putting up with your bullshit is exhausting."

Sylas laughed and Claire knew she was missing something. She hated knowing so little about the man who was starting to mean so much to her.

Thankfully, Kaya looked to her and said, "I'm sorry about the picture leaking. Kian believes it wasn't you, and I trust him. Hopefully being stuck with Mr. Grumpy Pants isn't too difficult."

Claire shook her head. "No, although I will admit it's happening a bit fast."

Kaya smiled. "Well, the opposite isn't much better. It took just over a decade for my male to finally get it right."

Sy sighed. "This again."

Kaya gave him an amused look. "Stop flirting with all the females and I may let it go."

Aidan grunted. "If you two want to flirt, Claire and I have other people to talk with."

Kaya's gaze moved to Aidan, her look serious. "Before you go, Sy and I may have an idea for your first secret event with the human public."

Claire asked, "What? I haven't even had a chance to think strategies with Kian. He said we could work together on this."

Kaya nodded. "We'll need your help, for sure. But the University of Washington in Seattle is hosting their annual Shifter Appreciation Week in two weeks and Sy knows one of the organizers and has asked for some speakers. They wish to hold an indoor event. Only a certain amount of people will be admitted, all of whom should be vetted supporters." Kaya looked from Claire to Aidan and back again. "Provided, of course, you're willing."

Claire was smart enough to realize a good opportunity when she heard it. Holding grudges or resenting someone for accomplishing something without your help was petty and damaging to her cause. "Well, if Kian says it's okay and there's a plan in place to get me there without getting arrested, I don't see why not."

Aidan chimed in, "I don't know if it's the best idea. Even with a secure plan to transport you to the university and back, you haven't had any self-defense training and you're going to need it in case any of the anti-shifter groups, especially Human Purity, show up."

Sy interjected, "But it's an invite-only event, where shifters and humans from all over the area will attend. In addition to organizer security, DarkStalker and GreyFire would help protect your female." Sy paused a second and his eyes became serious. "I wouldn't ask you, Aidan, if I didn't trust the person in charge."

Claire sensed Aidan's resistance loosening. She just needed to convince him a little bit more. "Us together and presenting a united front, despite the risk of getting caught, will help verify our love story. We may not have many chances to do it, so we should take every opportunity we can before it's impossible."

Aidan studied her in silence. Kaya's voice was gentle when she said, "You can't keep her in a cage, Aidan. With all of the security planned, she'll be nearly as safe as if she were still here."

Claire held her breath, waiting for Aidan's answer. If he said no, she wasn't sure what to do.

Letting out a sigh, Aidan finally gave his answer. "You're right, keeping Claire in a cage is like trying to keep a shifter locked up in a zoo; it would drive her crazy." He tightened his grip on Claire's side. "However, you need to promise me that from now until the event, you'll train every day with me no matter how sore you are or how much you hate it."

Claire tilted her head. "Only if you agree to let me talk with some possible supporters without you at my side, scaring them shitless with your glares and world-famous grunts."

"As long as I think it's safe, then fine," Aidan answered. "We'll start training tomorrow. Sy, Kaya, once you clear it with Kian, send us all the information you have. Also, ensure with your contact that DarkStalker and GreyFire can help with security. If they say no, then we're not going."

Sy's winks and grins were gone, replaced with a seriousness that made him look even more like his twin brother. "It shouldn't be a problem. They've been trying to get me to go for years, but this is the first time I thought it worth attending."

Aidan opened his mouth, but Kaya beat him to it. "Enough planning for now, you two. Tonight is critical in gaining support for Aidan and Claire's claiming and eventual mating." She leaned into Sy's side. "Besides, you owe me a dance and I'm claiming it now."

Despite the fact no one was dancing, Sy and Kaya bid farewell, found an empty corner, and began dancing.

Aidan's voice garnered her attention. "Sy used to be my boss. He might be a charming flirt, but he's devoted to Kaya. Only a fool in love would dance in a room where no one else was dancing."

It was on the tip of Claire's tongue to ask Aidan if he'd ever done it with his former mate, but a group of younger shifters approached and started asking Claire questions. As she tried her best to win them over while remaining truthful, all thoughts of dancing, love, or even possible danger in two weeks' time fled her mind.

Thankfully, her years of being friendly and winning support for the SEA proved useful as they worked the room. While any one of the shifters in the clan could turn on her or gossip behind her back, Claire felt confident she had a good start. After all, she'd learned long ago she couldn't win over everyone.

The older shifters in the back of the room glared in her direction, but with Aidan at her side, she didn't care. Given what she knew of Kian, she should be safe.

Only time would tell if her gut was correct or not.

CHAPTER FIFTEEN

Two weeks after the claiming ceremony, Aidan pulled into their assigned parking spot at the University of Washington's or, as the locals called it, U-Dub's campus and switched off his car. Turning to Claire, his eyes darted to her V-neck sweater and frowned. "I still wish you would've worn a higher cut top."

She rolled her eyes. "This again? My sweater barely shows any cleavage, which is quite an accomplishment considering I have a lot of it."

Remembering earlier in the morning, when Claire's breasts were in his hands as he took her nipple deep into his mouth made his cock twitch to life. Then his cougar pushed to take her one more time. She had on a skirt. They could manage it with no one seeing.

Stop it, cat. No one is going to take her away from us.

With a huff, his inner cougar receded, allowing Aidan control of his mind again. "The necklace draws the eye."

Claire touched the large, simple onyx stone hanging on a silver chain. "But you gave it to me. I thought you'd approve."

"I do, but not outside of the clan. There, at least, I know no one will take you because you're thoroughly laced with my scent."

She raised an eyebrow. "To a passerby, that would sound kind of creepy." When he growled, Claire grinned. "Oh, come on. I've at least helped ease some of your nervousness about your upcoming speech."

Rather than admit it, Aidan unlocked the doors. "We should probably go if we're to meet Dani and her security team on time."

They exited the car. Without a word, Claire came to his side and the instant he felt her warmth against him, both man and beast calmed a fraction. Things had gone well over the last two weeks, but almost too well. There hadn't been any more photos leaked to the press, let alone threats from Human Purity. Not even the anti-human leaning members of his clan had stirred up trouble. At least, not in public. Kian had taken care of them and somehow eased all of their doubts.

And while the authorities had done a few fly-bys over DarkStalker's land, they had yet to try to take Claire away. However, that could all change at the upcoming event, especially since Claire didn't carry any young, which meant she didn't have the same protections as the other human, Lauren. Unless the bears ever found a damn loophole, every second with Claire could be his last.

Then they entered one of the side thoroughfares running through the campus and Claire gasped, garnering his attention. "Look at the cherry blossoms. I was afraid it was too late and we'd miss them."

Glancing at the light pink blossoms that formed an almost canopy over their heads, he tried to understand his female's wonder. At least, he could tell no one lurked in the trees. "I guess they're pretty, although I prefer evergreens draped in snow."

"Why, Aidan Scott, you can be romantic."

He looked down to find Claire grinning. "You keep saying that as if it's a surprise. I somehow think you do it to tease me."

She gave an innocent look. "Who, me? I don't know what you're talking about. I never tease anyone."

Smiling, he bent his head to kiss her nose. "I'll save my teasing for later, when you're naked."

"Oh, you haven't seen anything yet in that department, Mr. Cougar. I'm waiting until you tease me first, because mine will be much, much worse."

Snaking a hand around to her ass, he gave her a pat. "Later, my little human. Make it through this and I might reward you."

"Yes, because I'm the one not used to public speaking."

Claire had a point, but as they approached the lecture hall where the event was being held, Aidan focused on his surroundings, his cat on high alert. "I'll be fine. I've been practicing. However, for now, we need to keep our eyes open. Don't hesitate to use the training I showed you, okay? If we're separated, go to the secret meeting spot we discussed."

"I think you're trying to avoid saying I'm right, but okay. I will. There's Dani, so you shouldn't worry. If there's anyone we can trust, it's her."

He wished, but judging by Dani's grim expression, something hadn't gone as planned. As soon as she was close enough, Dani said without preamble, "I just spoke to the head organizer, and apparently, he received threats from Human Purity. They might crash your speech and Q and A session." She looked to Aidan. "Are you sure you still want to go through with this? You know what happened to Sean and Lauren last December."

Sean and Lauren had been dating at the time, not yet mated. Since Sean was a cougar-shifter and Lauren a human, Human Purity had made them an example by kidnapping Sean. Only Lauren's love for her shifter had brought Sean back from his inner cat taking over for good.

Aidan looked down to Claire. If it were up to him, he would lock her away inside DarkStalker's mountain complex and never let her out. Yet if he did that, she would soon grow to hate him.

Instead of ordering Claire around, he asked his female, "What do you think? Should we still go through with it?"

His cat snarled, urging them to take her back to the car straightaway. He just about had his cat under control when Claire answered, "Yes. Otherwise, they will have won and I'll be damned if I lose to a bunch of crazies. This might be our only chance to meet with the public. I still think doing so will help the vote pass easier."

Aidan touched her chin. "You're going to turn my hair gray in no time, but hell if I don't love your strength, Claire Davis." His inner cougar kept snarling, but Aidan told his cat that Dani would keep them safe. Once the beast calmed a fraction, he added, "Just don't get yourself killed and stay on high alert. If I think there's a credible threat, we're leaving."

She eyed him a second and nodded. "As much as I want to beat the bastards, I don't want to die."

Caressing her lower lip with his thumb, he murmured, "Good, because I can't imagine life without you."

He'd been waiting to tell how he really felt, but this wasn't the time to share feelings. He hoped she wouldn't choose now to discuss them in depth.

Claire smiled at him, her eyes full of tenderness, before she looked to Dani. "Tell the organizer we're still going through with it. Maybe have some of the organizer's security people blend into the crowd. As much as I trust you guys to protect us, shifters tend to stand out in a crowd of humans."

Aidan nodded. "Do as she says, but still have our people around. Some of the Human Purity cowards might steer clear of a real-life shifter, especially with glares and growls."

"As much as I want to whisk you two back to DarkStalker, the two suggestions combined should hopefully minimize the risk," Dani said before motioning toward the lecture hall. "I'll make sure everything is in place. Give me ten minutes. If I think the room unsafe, we're leaving."

Aidan nodded, a small part of him wanting there to be a threat so Claire wouldn't be put at risk.

Once Dani left, Aidan stared down at his mate-to-be and murmured, "Be strong, but not rash, Claire, and we should be fine."

~~~

Most people would be offended at Aidan's remarks, but over the last two weeks, she'd learned to appreciate her shifter's honesty. Hell, if more people acted like Aidan, the world would solve problems a lot quicker.

Patting his chest, she answered, "I know my limitations pretty well. I'm still sore in a few places."

"Well, good. Cockiness gets people killed."

Since they had a few minutes, Claire leaned against Aidan's side and he hugged her close. Breathing in his scent of male and forest, under the cherry blossoms, it felt as if she were in a dream, much like the last two weeks had been.

She couldn't imagine living anywhere but DarkStalker. Sure, she may not be in charge of the SEA any longer, but Kian listened to her ideas and used more than a few of her strategies. She was helping shifters achieve equality from the inside, and she loved it.

Of course, waking up to Aidan in his cougar form would occasionally startle her, but then she would curl next to her big kitty and fall asleep to his purrs. Once in a while, even Chloe would show up in their bed in her cougar form. With a big cat at her front, and a little cat at her back, she'd never feel cold again.

The upcoming event had brought reality back in a flash, though. She might be brave on the outside, but on the inside, her stomach was doing flips.

As if he could read her mind, Aidan rubbed her side as he said, "I believe in you, Claire. If you're attacked, your muscles are starting to remember the moves without thought. Besides, I'll be right there next to you. Not to mention Dani and the other shifter soldiers."

"I know, but I can't help thinking you'll be taken away from me. Two weeks is nowhere near enough."

"We have our whole lives, Claire. I would mate you right now, if you wanted."

She looked up, but there was nothing but sincerity and tenderness in his eyes. "You have the worst timing, Aidan Scott."

"So that means yes?"

"Not right now. I want to make sure Chloe is okay with it first."

Aidan's expression turned soft. He looked like he wanted to say something, but instead, he merely kissed her gently on the lips. "I guess that means we need to survive this thing. Otherwise, they'll have to face Chloe Scott, and they have no idea what she'll come up with."

Claire laughed. "I somehow doubt a seven-year-old can take down Human Purity."

"Oh, I bet if she put her mind to it and used those big eyes of hers, she could persuade enough people to help her."

She turned in his arms until she leaned against his chest. "Maybe next year, we can bring Chloe here to see the cherry blossoms. While you may not be impressed, I think she'll love them."

Aidan caressed her cheek. "That sounds like a plan."

Her man leaned down to kiss her, but Dani's voice interrupted them. "Sorry, love birds, but it's show time."

As they followed Dani into the lecture hall and down the corridor, Claire's heart pounded. Maybe she should turn away and flee back to DarkStalker so she wouldn't have to worry about anyone taking Aidan away from her.

Then she remembered her Aunt Gwen. Currently, the polls showed a fifty-fifty chance of the law passing. If Claire didn't do something drastic, such as talk with a live audience, then she could lose the vote and never see her aunt again.

No. Between Aidan, Dani, and everyone else, she should be safe. Claire would win the vote and hopefully see her aunt in the New Year. While the federal government looked as if they would turn a blind eye to shifter marriage equality in the states, even though it technically violated federal law, they could always change their minds.

They reached their entrance and everyone stopped. With a nod, Dani entered first. A few seconds later, she motioned for them to follow.

Taking a deep breath, Claire allowed Aidan to enter first and then her. Inside was a giant college lecture hall, full of people. Some of them were even holding up signs of support. One said, "Human-Shifter Love is also Precious" while another read, "Everyone Deserves a Happy Ending". A few people were also waving extra-large versions of the Shifter Equality Alliance flag.

Since the event was not only invite-only but also part of Shifter Appreciation Week, Claire had expected support. But unlike all the other events and speeches she'd given over the years, this one was personal. Their support actually touched her heart, giving her hope she could remain with Aidan for as long as she liked without fear of arrest, or worse.

They stopped at the side of the stage at the front of the room, near the stairs. Dani looked to her and Aidan. "I've done as much as I can to protect you two, but there's always a risk of danger. Keep an eye out and don't be afraid to cut the speech and questions short. Staying alive is more important than earning a few votes." Dani stared Claire down. "I'm talking to you, missy. Understand?"

Claire didn't back down. "I have common sense, Dani. Otherwise, I wouldn't have lasted this long."

Dani's expression softened a fraction. "I know, but Aidan is one of my oldest friends and I can't stand the thought of him losing someone else."

"I know," Claire answered. "I'll be careful, I promise."

Dani looked to Aidan. "You, too. Give the signal if you suspect anything."

Aidan gave a mock salute. "Yes, ma'am."

Rolling her eyes, Dani muttered, "I almost wish you'd be grumpy again."

With that, Dani melted into the crowd and a man spoke up on stage. "Our next speakers are quite a treat. While you knew it would be someone from the SEA, what you didn't know was that we have the former president of the SEA, Claire Davis, and her shifter fiancé, Aidan Scott, here today. Let's give them a warm welcome for being brave enough to come here and give their first talk in public together."

As the crowd applauded, the organizer motioned for Claire and Aidan to come up on stage. Threading her fingers through Aidan's, they made their way to the podium. Since Claire was the experienced speaker, they had agreed for her to give an introduction.

After receiving the all-clear from Dani on the side, Claire leaned toward the microphone. "Good afternoon, everyone. Thanks for inviting us to speak. Unfortunately, those who are expecting my man to walk around naked before shifting will be sorely disappointed. I'll just say that the photo doesn't do him justice." A few laughs broke out. "In all seriousness, we really do appreciate the invite and your support. I've been fighting for shifter and human marriage equality for nearly a decade, but now that I've found my own shifter, it's more than doing what's right—it's about finding my own happily ever after."

Cheers went up and Aidan squeezed her hand. After sharing a glance with her shifter, Claire spoke up again. "Now, the world has heard me speak a thousand times before, so to give you something new, Aidan will say a few words. Then I'll have a lot more words to say and take questions. Are you ready?"

Leaning forward, she cupped her ear and the crowd screamed yes. With a smile, she stepped to the side, allowing Aidan to take her place.

For a few seconds, he looked around the crowd and then he recited the words they'd rehearsed earlier. "Five years ago, illegal poachers killed my mate and our two unborn children. I never thought I would find someone again. Then Claire appeared in my life and now I can't imagine my life without her."

The crowd awed and Claire couldn't help but smile. Aidan didn't like sharing personal details, but she'd finally worn him down. Without personal details, voters wouldn't support their cause.

As soon as she placed her free hand over their clasped hands, Aidan continued. "However, that can all be taken away from me if voters don't approve the initiative to make shifter-human marriage legal in the State of Washington. I don't care what your politics are. This issue is nonpartisan. Just imagine if you couldn't marry someone because of their ethnicity. It was that way decades ago, but now it's unthinkable that interracial couples can't be together. I'm asking for you to see shifters and humans in the same light."

He paused and claps sounded out. One of the SEA flag holders waved his flag enthusiastically. So far, so good.

Aidan's voice boomed over the speakers again. "Most of you are already supporters, but we also need you to talk to your friends, families, and coworkers. We have a little over seven months to try to change the world. Let's help make Washington State the first in the country."

More applause and cheers went up, not that Claire could blame them. For all Aidan's protesting about public speaking, he was pretty good at it. Maybe not as good as her, but with a little more practice, he just might be.

One of the giant SEA flags stopped waving and she smiled. She knew from experience those things could be damn heavy.

The holder rested the base on the ground, the material of the flag covering his body. She was about to step to the podium for her turn when something rod-shaped poked briefly through the material. Wanting to be safe and not chance it, she released Aidan's hand and pushed him away.

The instant she was about to duck down, a shot fired and a burning sensation ripped through her side. A cacophony of screams, shouts, and running filled her ears as she fell to the stage. For a very long second, the world went still.

Then Aidan leaned down into her line of sight and cupped her face.

Resisting the Cougar

Pain wracking her body, Claire tried to focus on Aidan's words as he said, "Stay with me, Claire, do you hear? Don't fall asleep."

Yet her eyes grew heavy as she grew colder. She tried to keep her eyes open, but it took too much effort. She managed to whisper, "Aidan," before the world went black.

Chapter Sixteen

Aidan cradled Claire's head as her body went limp. For a split second, he believed she was dead. But then he noticed the slight rise and fall of her chest.

Claire was still alive.

Thank fuck. He couldn't lose her, not when he'd just found her.

Dani appeared next to him and examined Claire. His friend was often the clan's field medic, so he forced himself to lay Claire's head down and move out of the way.

As Dani worked her magic, ripping material and tying it tightly over the wound, both man and cat felt an ache in their heart. If Claire died right in front of them, Aidan wasn't sure he could survive the loss of someone else he loved.

Yes, he loved his human, yet he'd never told her. She needed to live so he could tell her a million times over how much she'd come to mean to him. Claire was not only his second chance, but Chloe's as well.

Chloe. Thank fuck his daughter was back on DarkStalker's land. Watching Claire being shot would've devastated her. As much as he didn't like hiding things from his daughter, he would keep the severity of Claire's injuries a secret. There was no use in scaring Chloe unnecessarily.

Thinking of his daughter helped to settle Aidan's shock. He was useless as a medic, so he chanced a look at the crowd to see if the shifter soldiers needed his help. However, both human security and volunteers from DarkStalker and GreyFire had a few humans restrained and face down on the ground. The one who'd shot Claire had three shifters restraining him.

If he were to hazard a guess, the man was with Human Purity.

Without thinking, he whispered, "I never should have let her talk me into this."

Dani's no-nonsense voice answered him. "Don't fucking play the blame game, Aidan Scott. I need you focused. Apply pressure here while I check her vitals."

Aidan snapped into soldier mode and tried to imagine Claire as one of his men or women. He failed utterly, but he still managed to press against the compress on her wound. "Tell me straight, Dani. Will she live?"

Dani met his eyes, her expression neutral. "I don't know. There's a GreyFire doctor on site and on standby just in case, and she should be here soon. She can tell you more."

The GreyFire wolves were known for their medical research. Some of their researchers had also received top-notch training at some of the best medical schools.

He was about to ask who was on site when Lisa, the GreyFire doctor in question, wedged in next to Claire. Behind Lisa, two other wolf-shifters carried a stretcher between them. Lisa did a check and then motioned for her team to get Claire on the stretcher.

Aidan couldn't take the suspense any longer. "Will she live?"

Lisa's voice was steady. "I won't know for certain until I get her to GreyFire's nearby lab. But I will do everything within my power to save her, Aidan. That I will promise you." Lisa looked to Dani. "If the human authorities show up, stall them as long as you can. They might try to take Claire if they find out who she is."

Dani nodded as the two wolf-shifters moved down the stage, carrying Claire. Aidan took a step to follow. Lisa put up a hand. "You can only come with us if you can keep your cat under control. I can't try to save Claire's life and deal with your alpha possessive bullshit. Can you do that?"

Aidan's cat snarled and clawed to take control. They should be with their female and make sure there weren't any other threats. The wolves weren't to be trusted.

Shut up. They are our best chance. Nodding, Aidan answered, "I can."

"Then come with me."

Aidan glanced to Dani, who motioned for him to go. "We've got this. The bastard who shot Claire is in custody and there's no fucking way I'm allowing him to escape. I'll handle the human authorities. Take care of your mate."

Rather than argue about Claire not yet being his mate, he nodded and went to catch up to Lisa and the two other wolves.

As he fought the memories of the past and the last time his female had been shot, Aidan followed the woman he hoped would be his future for many years to come.

~~~

Five hours later, Aidan paced up and down the length of a small room. Lisa had been operating the whole time, and it'd been hours since the last update. Every second that ticked by was another stab to his heart. He had no fucking idea if a long surgery was a good or bad thing. All he knew was Claire hadn't died yet.

But what if she did? Aidan's cougar snarled, wanting to do something to help. She couldn't die. She was their fire.

Aidan ran a hand through his hair. He hated being so useless. After this, he didn't care if he had to chain Claire to the bed; he wasn't allowing her off DarkStalker's land until he could guarantee her safety.

As he continued to pace, the silence only made him relive Claire getting shot over and over again inside his head. He would never forget the sight of her falling to the ground or her blood soaked shirt.

Aidan had been so damn focused on getting his speech right that he hadn't paid enough attention to his surroundings, leaving Claire to protect him. With training, he could see her taking on the world, but she wasn't ready and Claire had paid the price for his short-sightedness.

He would spend the rest of his life proving to Claire and Chloe that he could be depended upon.

The door opened, thankfully interrupting his thoughts. At the sight of Dani's familiar face, he sighed. "Did they send you here to handle me?"

She raised an eyebrow. "No, although I'm well aware of you being a dick for the last few hours. I would tell you none of this is their fault, but you wouldn't listen. So I'll just ask if you're willing to listen to the news I have."

"What news?"

"I'm going to take that as a yes, you'll listen. So, sit."

Dani was one of the few who could order him around. Exhausted from worry and pacing, he sat without a fight, grateful for a mini-distraction. "I'm sitting, so tell me. But make it quick, in case the doctor comes in with news."

She gave him a sympathetic look and nodded. "One of the ShadowClaw bears is here and wants to discuss your options regarding Claire."

'If she survives' was left unsaid.

Pushing aside the negative thought, Aidan focused on the possibility he could live with Claire without fear of the authorities taking her away from him. "Tell me the options."

Dani frowned. "The bastard won't tell me anything. He says he needs to tell you and Kian at the same time."

"But Kian is back on DarkStalker's land."

She put up a hand. "One of the wolves is fetching a tablet and patching through a connection."

"And the bear?"

She pointed a thumb toward the door. "Waiting just outside."

Talking business with Dani brought back some of his logical mind. "What does your cat's instinct say? Do you think we can trust him?"

"Even without my gut, you've heard the name Nathan Carter before. He's apparently the second-in-command of ShadowClaw these days."

Nate Carter had not only served in the Shifter Division of the US Army and won a medal of honor in Iraq, he'd been a champion boxer. A decade ago, Aidan had wanted nothing more than the chance to box with the bear.

Then he'd met Emily, and she had tamed his cat. "You know I have, but what's he doing here? He was banned from leaving the Cascades for fighting one too many times in the human bars."

Dani shrugged. "I don't really care why he ventured off ShadowClaw's land as long as he can help us. Can I just let him in so we can find a way for you to keep Claire? I want to send him home as soon as possible."

Dani's voice almost sounded irritated, which piqued Aidan's curiosity since Dani was as steady as they came. "Why, did he push some of your buttons?"

"Let him in and you'll see firsthand how his other reputation is true as well."

Despite everything that was going on, Aidan nearly smiled. "He hit on you."

She rolled her eyes. "More like he wanted a quickie. Something about his inner bear waking up after a sleepy winter."

Part of him wanted to hear more, but Aidan finally just motioned toward the door. His future with Claire was more important; he refused to believe she'd die. "Let him in. If there's a way to keep Claire with me always, I want to put it into place straight away."

"Fine, but I've warned him to keep his hands and eyes to himself. If he doesn't, I'll kick him in the balls."

"Can you wait to do that until after he tells me a way to keep Claire with me?"

Dani harrumphed. "I'll try, but I can't make any promises."

As Dani went to the door, Aidan resisted the urge to tease her. Not just because of Claire's condition, but also because few males dared to flirt with Danika Fisher because of her rank. Aidan was curious to see the infamous bear fighter and how he treated one of his oldest friends.

Opening the door, Dani motioned for Nate to enter.

The bear was older than Aidan remembered, with a few lines around his eyes and mouth and some gray hair mixed into the brown. But the strong jaw and the nose broken a few too many times were the same. Nate's green eyes met his briefly before latching onto Dani. Nate's deep voice filled the small room. "You know locking me out only made my bear more anxious to see you again, Dani. My offer still stands."

Dani rolled her eyes. "One of my clan members was shot and is in surgery. Have a little tact. I'm sure your cock will last until this evening, when you can find some female to fuck."

The corner of Nate's mouth ticked up. "I love a female who isn't afraid to swear. Cats really are feisty. I think you need a strong, protective bear to help calm your cougar."

Judging by the look in Dani's eyes, she was about to clock the bear. Aidan stood up and interjected, "I'd leave her alone for now. Besides, you have information we could use."

Nate met his gaze and his eyes assessed him before saying, "I'm sorry about your female. I truly am, but I won't disobey my orders. I'll tell you once your clan leader joins us."

Aidan didn't back down. "But there is a way, then?"

Nate shook his head. "Not even offering me your delicious redheaded friend would make me talk, although I would be sorely tempted." He grinned at Dani. "Are you sure I can't have just one taste of your sweet lips?"

From the corner of his eye, he saw Dani narrow her eyes. "Ask to taste me again, I dare you."

Thankfully, there was a knock on the door and Aidan answered it. It was one of the wolves he couldn't name. The male wolf handed him a tablet. "The connection is live."

With a nod, Aidan took it and shut the door. Looking down, he saw his clan leader and said, "Sorry, Kian, but ShadowClaw won't talk without you taking part."

Kian answered, "No worries. I'm more concerned about you. You seem calmer and more levelheaded than I've heard in my reports."

"The possibility of keeping Claire has calmed both man and cat temporarily," Aidan answered. "Can we just start the meeting?"

Kian nodded. "Turn me toward the bear."

Aidan complied and Nate bobbed his head before saying, "It's been a while, Kian."

"I don't think I've seen you since my teenage days when I bested you in a fight."

Nate raised his brows. "I've filled out since then. You wouldn't stand a chance."

Impatient, Aidan jumped in. "I'm sorry to break up the memories, but can we find out how to keep Claire with me, without fear of the police arresting her?"

Nate shrugged. "Fine. It's pretty simple, really. I'm sure you've heard of the Witness Protection Program used by the FBI?"

"Yes," Aidan answer. "But what does that have to do with Claire?"

"Sometimes, they place humans with shifters for protection."

Dani frowned. "Since when? That would violate a number of human laws, and they certainly haven't asked DarkStalker to help."

Nate moved his gaze to Dani. "ShadowClaw helped once about thirty years ago. Since the human has long left our care, I'm not breaking any rules by telling you that much."

Dani demanded, "Why wait this long to tell us? You know we have another human on our land. This information would've been helpful."

Before Nate could answer, Kian interjected, "That's all in the past and I only care about the present. Even if what you say is true, the FBI reached out to the bears. How can that help Claire and Aidan? I highly doubt they'll just magically appear at our doorstep and offer such a deal."

Nate turned back toward the tablet. "It took a few weeks of digging and bribing some other bears across the country, but we found a buried sub-article to a law written several decades ago that can help and most likely keep the human on your land. However, that information comes with a price."

Kian raised his brows. "What does Odessa want in exchange for that information?"

"My clan leader wants a face-to-face meeting with you and Kaya Alexie. She'll make her request there."

Kian paused before finally saying, "I don't like agreeing to blind favors."

Nate replied, "She assured me nothing would hurt your clan or any of your clan members. The meeting wouldn't be until summer, because of scheduling reasons. But Odessa trusts you to honor your word."

Kian paused a second before giving a curt nod. "I can only speak for my clan and not Kaya's, but I will meet with your leader. However, if her favor involves harming my clan, I won't agree to it."

Nate nodded. "She expected as much. Tell GreyFire about the meeting and to contact me with their answer. I'll leave my contact information here before I leave."

Aidan had been patient, but couldn't hold back any longer. "So what's the law that will allow me to keep my female?"

Nate jumped right in. "When a human has been attacked or turns state's evidence against a terrorist group or some sort of organized crime unit, they can ask the federal government for help to ensure their safety. Since shifters are notoriously protective, if a human knows a local clan and can gain their approval, he or she can be placed with them. Not even the mob wants to start a war with a shifter clan."

Aidan frowned. "This goes against every law I know of."

The bear-shifter shrugged. "It took my clan weeks to find it, so it's not exactly broadcasted. Hell, the FBI probably forgot it even exists. It was written in the 1970s to aid the RICO Act, which was used to take down mobsters."

"So a law used to fight mobsters is going to allow me to keep my female?"

Nate crossed his arms over his massive chest. "It shouldn't matter how the law originated as long as it helps you."

Aidan's opinion of Nate went up a notch. "True. And your lawyers have given the green light to using the old law?"

"Yes. Unless a new law is passed to repeal it, the law still stands. My clan will email all the information you need in the next few hours and offer assistance, provided Kian keeps his word."

Kian's voice answered, "I will. I don't know how to contact Odessa personally since she eschews technology, so thank your clan leader for me."

Nate uncrossed his arms. "Sure thing. Now, I need to go." He looked over to Dani. "I'm sure I'll see you in the summer, Danika Fisher. I look forward to it."

Before anyone could say a word, Nate Carter was gone.

Aidan turned the tablet around to speak with his clan leader. "Keep me updated on the validity of the law, Kian. I'm in no state to read and decode political jargon."

"No problem. You stay with Claire as long as you need, okay? GreyFire is helping with our security until you two are back."

Aidan glanced to Dani, who shrugged. "I'm staying here to help you. I trust Sylas to keep DarkStalker safe."

Since Sylas was Kian's twin brother and former second-in-command, Aidan trusted Sy as well.

Aidan was about to ask for an update on the attackers when someone knocked on the door and entered. It was Lisa.

Handing the tablet to Dani, he walked over the wolf. "How is she?"

"Claire survived the surgery, but she lost a lot of blood and her heart stopped once. It's beating steady for now, however, so I'm optimistic."

Ignoring the pain in his heart, he asked, "Can I see her?"

Lisa smiled. "Yes, although she's unconscious." The doctor's face turned stern. "If you try to wake her before she's ready, I will ban you from her room, cougar."

"I won't wake her up, I promise. I just want to see her and hold her hand."

Lisa's expression eased. "Good, then follow me."

As Aidan and Lisa walked down one corridor and then another, his heart pounded harder. Claire was alive, and if he had any say in it, she would stay that way.

The wolf-shifter finally stopped in front of a door and whispered, "She'll need your strength. Even though she's unconscious, you need to help her fight for her life. She's human, which means her recovery will be trickier without shifter healing abilities."

He nodded impatiently. "Stubbornness is my middle name."

"Good."

As the wolf doctor opened the door to Claire's room, Aidan braced himself and went inside.

Claire lay on the bed with a few wires and tubes attached to her. She was breathing on her own, but she was pale. Without her glasses or the vitality of her personality, he barely recognized his female.

Slowly, Aidan went to the bed and sat down. Taking Claire's hand, he brought it to his lips and kissed it. The door clicked closed behind him and he whispered, "Fight for your life, Claire Davis, because I love you and want to mate you. Not only that, you have work left to do for all shifter-kind. Dying is not an option, understand?"

Claire remained motionless except for the slow rise and fall of his chest. Placing her hand on his cheek, he willed his strength and health to transfer to her.

CHAPTER SEVENTEEN

A singing voice filtered into Claire's mind, creating a mosaic of colors and shapes to match the tune. As they swirled around, shrinking and expanding, she deciphered some of the singing.

One shifter, two shifter, three shifter, four. Embrace your inner cat and roar, roar, roar.

The voice sounded oddly familiar. If only she could place it.

Five shifter, six shifter, seven shifter, eight. Change your form and wait, wait, wait.

When the time is right, pounce on your prey before it's too late!

The words sounded like a nursery rhyme. Before she could think too hard, a familiar male voice said, "Why do you keep singing that tune over and over? Cougars can't even roar."

"But, Daddy, it's fun to say. I like pretending I'm a lion."

Cougars, Daddy, and a girl and man; it was Aidan and Chloe.

Claire tried opening her eyes, but they were heavy. Trying something easier, she moved a finger. When she moved another, there was a gasp and Chloe's voice shouted, "Daddy, look. Claire's moving. Maybe my singing helped."

A warm hand caressed her forehead. "Claire, are you awake? If you are, open your eyes for me, love."

The relief in Aidan's voice pushed Claire to try harder until her eyes opened a crack. Even without her glasses, Aidan's face was close enough she could see him perfectly. Even to her own ears, her voice was scratchy. "Aidan."

He kissed her on the lips and then her nose, his eyes shimmering with tears. "You're awake." He glanced over his shoulder. "Tell the guard outside that Claire is awake."

"But Daddy, I want to say hello to Claire too."

"Then hurry and tell the guard."

With a huff, she heard Chloe open the door. But Aidan's scratchy voice, full of emotion, caught her attention. "I should start by saying thank you for saving my life."

She tried to raise a hand to Aidan's face, but couldn't move her hand more than an inch or two off the bed. The slightest movements took more effort than it ever had before in her life.

Yet somehow, she made her voice work. "You would've done the same for me."

Aidan took one of her hands and squeezed, his warmth helping to chase away the cold. "I should have paid more attention, Claire. I failed you and totally understand if you want me to leave."

She squeezed his hand lightly. "You leave and I will kick your ass."

He smiled. "I'd like to see you try."

"Just shut up and give me a kiss."

Aidan pressed his lips against hers, slowly and gently tasting her lips. When he pulled away, she nearly asked for another, but then a fuzzy Chloe appeared on the other side of her bed. "Claire, I'm so happy you're awake! I've been practicing my paper flowers and I can't wait to show you how good I've gotten."

Claire smiled. "How about you give me a hug first."

Chloe gently laid her head on Claire's chest and stayed there. With Aidan caressing her forehead and Chloe's weight on her chest, she felt at home.

While blurry, a woman with short, blonde hair she didn't recognize appeared at her bedside. Aidan nodded toward the woman. "This is Dr. Lisa. She's a GreyFire wolf and the woman who saved your life."

Claire tried her best to focus on the fuzzy shape. "Thank you, Doctor."

"I'm just happy you made it. Between Kian, Kaya, Aidan, and the SEA breathing down my neck, you being alive makes my life easier."

Claire heard the teasing in the woman's voice, but wished she could see her. "You didn't by chance save my glasses as well?"

Aidan chuckled, released her hand, and slowly put a pair of glasses on her face. Everything went back into focus.

The doctor smiled down at her and said, "I need to examine you, but I'll give you a few minutes with your family first while I check the readings on the machines. They've pretty much lived in this room for the past three days."

Claire blinked. "I was out for three days?"

Lisa nodded. "Yes, and it's going to be a long recovery with plenty of physical therapy. You aren't going to be making any speeches any time soon, I'm afraid. Aidan will have to take care of you until you're stronger."

While tired, Claire felt more like herself and couldn't resist saying, "A man waiting on me hand and foot? I think I could get used to that." Lisa laughed as Aidan grunted. Looking at her man, she added, "It's not like you won't be hovering anyway. Shifter males are notorious for hovering around a sick mate."

He caressed her forehead some more. "Yes, we just need to make the mate part official first."

Chloe chimed in with a squeal. "Yay! I was hoping you'd be my new mommy, Claire. And maybe once you're better, you can give me a little brother. Or, sister, although a brother would be cuter."

Claire started to laugh but then groaned. Aidan's voice was tender when he spoke, "Are you all right, Claire? Where does it hurt?"

Pain throbbed in her left side. "My left side, which I'm guessing is where I was shot."

Dr. Lisa pushed Aidan out of the way, pulled back the blanket, and gently felt her side. With a nod, Lisa put the blanket back. "You're tender but not swollen, which is a good sign. What you need more than anything is rest."

Claire eyed Aidan. "I'll only rest if you promise to do the same." He opened his mouth, but she beat him to it. "The circles under your eyes tell me all I need to know. Get some sleep, Aidan. I'll be here when you wake up."

"I would argue, but I have a feeling I'd lose."

Claire glanced to Chloe. "Can I put you in charge of making sure your dad gets some sleep?"

Chloe bobbed her head. "Yes, Claire. I'll do a good job and make sure he takes a nap."

"Thanks, Chloe. And maybe when I wake up, you can show me your flowers."

"Of course. I'm going to decorate your room and surprise you."

Claire smiled. "I can hardly wait."

Lisa cut in. "Okay, you two, out. I'll look after Claire and let you know when she wakes up. Jose is waiting outside the door to show you to one of the temporary quarters our researchers use whenever they pull all-nighters."

Aidan kissed her gently. "Sleep well and heal, love. We have lots to discuss when you wake up."

She frowned. "Why would you mention that now? I'll be wondering what the hell you need to say."

One corner of his mouth ticked up. "It's good news, Claire. I found a way for you to stay with me and Chloe, always, if that's what you want. But you need to sleep first. If the doctors tell me you fight it and don't get some rest, I'll wait longer to tell you the news."

She sighed. "Fine. But I'm only giving in easily because I'm not at full strength. Don't expect this to be a regular thing."

Aidan grinned. "I wouldn't dream of it." He kissed her again. "Sweet dreams, love."

Chloe kissed her cheek. "See you soon, Claire. I'm glad you're okay."

Claire smiled. "Me, too, Chloe, me too."

Once Aidan and Chloe left, Lisa gave her some water. Then she stated, "I'm going to give you something to make you sleep because if I were you, I'd be wondering what the hell Aidan was teasing about, too."

"Do you know what it is?"

Lisa shook her head. "Not really, just that the bears found a way to legally allow you to stay with DarkStalker. It's very hush-hush, though, so I'm not in the loop."

The doctor took out a needle, placed it into the IV opening, and pushed some drugs into her system. Before the drugs could knock her out, she murmured, "Thanks, Doctor, for keeping me alive."

She heard, "Don't thank me, your spirit is something else, especially for a human," before the world went black.

~~~

Aidan checked his reflection in the mirror one more time and brushed his hair to the side.

Chloe put her hand in his. "You look good, Daddy. You always tell me if I play too much with my hair, it will fall out and I don't know if I want a bald daddy just yet."

With a grin, he placed a hand on Chloe's head. "So what do you think? I want to look nice for Claire."

His daughter nodded. "I almost don't recognize you. You usually don't brush your hair or wear nice shirts."

Aidan smoothed his button-up shirt. "Don't worry, I feel trapped in this thing and it's coming off as soon as possible, but Claire deserves it."

Chloe released his hand and leaned against the bathroom counter. "Are you sure I can't go with you? I have some real flowers to give Claire and the longer I wait, the more they'll die."

He crouched down until he was eye level. "The flowers will last another half a day. This one time, I need to go alone. I'll take you to visit Claire tomorrow, okay?"

Chloe gave a dramatic sigh. "I guess. Just let her know that I didn't forget about her."

"I'll do that." Standing up, Aidan moved them out of the bathroom. "Just make sure to follow Dani's instructions tonight. I don't want to hear tales of you roaring inside your bedroom and playing lion-shifter."

"I'll try, but it's just so hard sometimes. I want to roar."

Thankfully, a knock prevented him from telling Chloe she couldn't change her animal shifter form based on desire.

Opening the door, he greeted his friend. "Thanks, Dani. You sure you can handle this?"

"I train young alphas all the time. I can handle one seven-year-old." Dani looked around Aidan at Chloe. "I can teach you more secret moves, if you want, Chloe?"

The little girl clapped her hands. "Ooh, I can't wait. Maybe I can be a sentry like you and Daddy."

Aidan opened his mouth, but Dani gave him a shove. "Go. You don't know how long Claire will stay awake this time."

"Fine, just stay out of trouble."

As the door shut behind him, he heard Chloe ask, "Can we invite some of the wolves over to play?"

Smiling at his daughter's willingness to accept anyone, regardless of shifter animal or if they were even human, he rushed down the hall. Dani had been right; he didn't know how long he had before Claire fell back asleep.

He'd slept nearly a day himself and felt rejuvenated. He hoped Claire was faring better.

The few minute walk seemed more like an eternity. Both man and cat desperately needed to hold their female close. Being apart for even a day when she was injured grated against his animal's instinct to protect their mate.

If not for Chloe, Aidan would've refused to leave Claire's side. But his daughter had toughed out the last few days with him and had needed the sleep. Caring for his child was the only thing which could persuade his cat to leave their mate's care to the wolves.

Finally, he reached Claire's door. Nodding to the GreyFire guard standing watch, he took a deep breath before entering the room.

Claire was sitting upright in her bed, reading a tablet in her hands. The sight of her awake and acting as if she hadn't just nearly died warmed his heart. His mate would live.

At the sound of the door, she looked up and smiled at him. "Aidan."

His name on her lips only made his cat more anxious to hold their female.

Still, Claire was recovering and he needed to be gentle. Moving to her bedside, he kissed her forehead as the door clicked shut behind him. "Are you up for a visit?"

"Perhaps, although any strenuous activities will have to wait a few weeks."

He growled. "I may be a shifter male, but I can control myself if need be."

She grinned. "If you say so."

Sitting on the edge of her bed, he cupped her cheek with one hand. "I've missed you, love."

"I've missed you, too, although I'm afraid to compliment you and boost your ego. I'm not sure I can handle it at full-strength just yet."

As he stared into Claire's green eyes and saw the spirit and vitality in them, his heart eased a little. "If you're well enough to tease me, then you're definitely out of danger. We'll have you back in top form in no time. Otherwise, I'll have to try to be extra nice and not growl. That's not easy to do."

She grinned. "Damn, and here I thought I would have a manservant for the foreseeable future." He frowned as Claire winked. "Don't worry, it's not like I would ask you to wear a butler's uniform or anything."

"Butler's uniform my ass. Those things look itchy."

Claire placed a hand over her heart. "Well, as much as I'd like to see you dressed to the nines, this ordeal has had something positive come out of it." She held up the tablet. "The shooting helped our campaign."

"Is that what you were reading? I haven't had a chance to check any of the news."

Frowning, she tilted her head. "How is that possible? Staring at my unconscious form for hours would've been beyond boring."

"I didn't want to miss you waking up. Although, I did have to take care of Chloe some of the time."

As his female stared at him, he gathered the courage to say what needed to be said. Yet as he opened his mouth, Claire beat him to it. "You are strong, caring, and fierce. When I first met you, I never expected to find my other half in a grumpy shifter male. I love you, Aidan Scott, and I want to mate you." He frowned and she asked, "What's wrong now?"

"I was about to tell you that I love you, and you stole my thunder."

One corner of her mouth ticked up. "Is that why you combed your hair?"

"I always comb my hair." Claire shook her head, but Aidan continued, "Enough with my hair. You're caring and smart with an unmatched dedication to making the world a better place." He leaned down and nuzzled her cheek. "You also brought me back to life, not to mention you're stubborn and sexy as hell. I love you, Claire Davis, and I will mate you any time you're ready."

"Oh, Aidan."

Moving his head, he kissed her. It took everything he had not to take the kiss deeper, but he wouldn't risk Claire injuring herself further.

When he pulled away, he stayed a few inches from her face. "So that's a yes, I take it?"

"Of course it's a yes. But since I'm not about to mate you wearing a hospital gown with my ass hanging out, it's going to have to wait until we can go back to DarkStalker. We should have the ceremony there."

He craned his neck. "I wouldn't mind seeing your ass."

She lightly smacked him. "Not right now. Besides, you still haven't told me how I can stay with you. While the ballot measure to legalize shifter-human marriages is now ten points ahead in the polls, even if it passes, that's a long time away. I'm guessing you found something else to help us until then."

After explaining what Nate had shared, Claire shook her head. "To think something like this has been around all this time. I wish I could've met with the bears."

"Well, they'll be around in the summer some time, so you'll get your chance then. But..."

"But what?"

"Just stay clear of Nate Carter. He will flirt with you and then I'll have to kick his ass."

Claire laughed. "It sounds like this Nate person is interested in Dani, so I should be safe."

"I can't see Dani with Nate. They would forever be challenging each other's authority and would kill each other before long."

"If you say so. I'm betting on a hook-up. Dani needs a strong male, and a bear-shifter could actually win against her, if he tried."

Aidan rubbed her back. "I'll take that bet. Dani will succeed in keeping him away."

His female put out a hand. "Shake on it. If I win, I can ask for a favor."

He put his hand in hers. "And if I win, I'll ask the same."

After releasing his hand, Claire scooted to the opposite edge of her bed. "Enough about bets. Come cuddle with me and tell me what Chloe's up to right now. And anything else that can help alleviate my boredom."

Settling next to his female, she laid her head on his chest. The weight of Claire against him as her scent filled his nose made a combination of possessiveness and contentment course through his body. "Don't worry, tomorrow Chloe will entertain you. Just ask her to play lion-shifter with you."

Claire looked up at him. "Only if I can be a wolf-shifter." He grunted and she grinned. "Hey, it would be fun. I've always wanted to howl."

"Even if you could howl and smelled like wet dog, I'd still love you."

"Maybe I should mention the wet dog comment to Kaya when we see her next."

He sighed. "How many weeks do we have until you're recovered again?"

"Enough that you're going to feel the full brunt of both my personality and imagination. You may change your mind about mating me by then."

He laid his cheek on her head. "Never, Claire Davis. I love every quirky and stubborn bit of you."

"I love you, too, alphaness and all." Claire tapped her fingers on his chest. "Now, how about I tell you my idea for a shifter TV reality show? One where a woman can take her pick from any type of shifter she likes..."

As Claire rambled on about her idea, her voice soothed both man and cat. Never in a million years had he expected to find his second chance at love in a human female who liked to give orders and dreamed of producing her own reality TV show.

Yet he couldn't imagine his life without her.

He only hoped her dream of human-shifter marriage equality came true and that the federal government would accept it. Not just because it was right, but also because he wanted Claire to legally be allowed to come and go from DarkStalker's lands. Sure, she would be protected under the modified Witness Protection Program, but without marriage equality, she would be trapped for the rest of her life.

Rubbing up and down his female's hip, he pushed aside his doubts. Aidan would do whatever it took to ensure the new law passed in November.

Once it did, he would marry his female in the human way. After that, the world would have to look out because his mate would never stop trying to change the world.

And there was nowhere Aidan would rather be than at her side.

EPILOGUE

January 3rd, Ten Months Later

Claire listened as the judge said, "I now pronounce you man and wife."

Her Aunt Gwen then kissed her new husband, Ben. Applause rose up as Claire's new uncle took the kiss deeper.

When the couple finally broke off the kiss and faced the crowd, Aunt Gwen sought her eyes. Claire nodded, leaned against Aidan, and murmured, "The first human and shifter couple has now been officially married in the State of Washington."

Aidan hugged her tightly. "It was nice of you to allow your aunt to be the first. Although, we'll have our own before too much longer. Stir-crazy is too tame a word for how you've been acting these last few months, ever since you were granted the special witness protection program status."

She sighed. "I know, but my aunt has been on the run for over a decade. She deserved to be first, especially since the federal government hasn't said a word about enforcing federal law over state law. My aunt can finally live her life in peace. We'll have ours soon enough."

Watching her aunt and uncle make their way down from the stage and into the crowd, Claire moved toward her aunt. When she was close enough, she enveloped her in a hug. "I'm so happy for you, Aunt Gwen."

Gwen leaned back and eyes the same shade as Claire's looked back at her with love. "It's all thanks to you, Claire. Your parents would be proud."

She nodded. "I know." Claire turned toward Ben the bear-shifter and opened her arms. "How about a hug?"

With a sigh, he hugged her, his deep voice rumbling. "Hugging in public isn't my thing, but I owe you that much at least."

Releasing her uncle, she took a step back to Aidan's side. "You'll just have to get used to it since you'll be around a lot more. I'm a big-time hugger."

Her aunt touched her arm. "I just wish we could've come back sooner to attend your mating ceremony."

Claire unconsciously brushed her thumb across her palm, where she'd cut her hand before gripping Aidan's cut hand. "To be honest, I was just trying not to faint. There's a reason I never wanted to be a doctor and cutting living flesh is it."

Her aunt chuckled. "Big, bad Ben turned green during ours."

Ben mumbled, "I'm a website designer, not a damn soldier."

Gwen opened her mouth, but Kian appeared next to them, a baby carrier in each hand. Claire frowned. "You really shouldn't bring three-month-old babies to a wedding."

Trinity then joined their circle, her third baby snuggled over her shoulder. "I thought my children should be present for such a historical event."

Kian's reply was dry. "No, you just couldn't find a babysitter you trusted to watch over them."

Trinity rubbed her baby's back. "There are plenty of people I trust, but the babies needed to be here."

Having lived the past ten months on DarkStalker's lands, Claire knew their bickering could go on for a while, so she jumped in. "Aunt Gwen, I'm taking up your time. You really need to mingle with the crowd and get to know your new clan. Now that you're married, we'll have plenty of time to catch up after your honeymoon period."

Claire gestured at the mixture of wolf, bear, and cougar-shifters inside DarkStalker's grand meeting space. Having all three Cascade Shifter clans in one place was quite a feat in and of itself considering what had happened over the summer.

Ben eyed the crowd. "Do we have to?" He looked down at Gwen. "I'd rather spend my time celebrating alone."

Gwen looped her arm through her mate's. "No, mister, not yet. All of these people went to such lengths to help us and put the wedding together. We owe it to them to show some gratitude."

Ben sighed. "Fine, then let's get it over with."

Aidan chuckled at Claire's side. "I understand how you feel, bear, but it's best to please the females of Claire and Gwen's families."

Ben murmured, "Don't I know it," before Gwen swatted his arm.

Claire patted Aidan's chest. "Glad to see you're on board. It's taken nearly a year to get you to admit pleasing me is the easier way to go." She grinned. "I plan to remind you of your admission every day."

Everyone laughed, and two of Kian and Trinity's children began crying. Kian nodded toward Gwen and Ben. "That's our cue to go. Congrats again you two."

"Thank you," Gwen replied, as Kian and Trinity headed toward the door to take care of their triplets.

Gwen and Ben thanked Claire again before moving toward the clan leaders of GreyFire and ShadowClaw.

When they were alone, Claire turned in Aidan's arms and stared up into his brown eyes. "I want our wedding to be simple and private. I spend a lot of time at the center of the media, so any break I can get would be fantastic."

Aidan patted her ass with one hand. "Good luck, love. You know Chloe wants chocolate fountains and some kind of light show."

Claire smiled. "She's taking her maid of honor gig a little too seriously."

"Well, at least she's not asking for a baby brother every other hour."

"True, although maybe we can fulfill her request next year, if my plans for California come to fruition. Just answer me one thing: you don't have twins or triplets in your family, do you?"

Aidan laughed. "No, although both are pretty common in shifter-shifter pairings."

"Good thing I'm human then. I have no idea how Kian balances triplets with his clan duties."

Her mate shrugged. "Kian is good at almost everything. Although I heard that Sy goes over to help a lot. Something about it being an uncle's duty to spoil his nieces and nephew."

Chloe raced up to them, Aidan's brother and his mate right behind her. Chloe jumped up and down. "Did you see it? It was so pretty! Daddy, you should marry Claire next, right here, in front of everyone."

Claire squeezed Chloe's shoulder. "There's a three-day waiting period for a marriage license, Chloe, so it's impossible. The law only started on January first."

Chloe slumped her shoulders. "I guess." She straightened up. "That just means I have more time to plan." She looked to Claire. "What do you think about the clan watching you get married in their animal forms? That would make a pretty cool picture."

Claire bit her lip. "If you can convince the clan, then I'm all in."

Chloe clapped her hands. "Yes! Then I'd better get started." Chloe looked to Aidan's brother. "Uncle Jeremy, will you help me?"

Jeremy looked less than enthusiastic, but his mate, Naomi, grinned and nodded. "I think it's a grand idea, Chloe. Who shall we ask first?"

"How about Kian? He's a nice, wild-looking cougar in his cat form."

To her credit, Naomi didn't laugh, but merely took hold of Chloe's shoulders and turned her around. "Okay, then, let's see if we can find him and ask. Maybe we can get Trinity on board, too."

As Naomi and Chloe dragged Jeremy off with them, Claire finally let out her laugh. When she finally caught her breath again, she looked up at Aidan. "I bet she manages it. And she's right; it would be a pretty cool picture."

Aidan shook his head. "I would say not to encourage her, but the two of you are like peas in a pod."

"Aw, is my shifter man feeling left out?" Claire placed her hands on his chest. "Since your brother and Naomi are watching Chloe, we could sneak out and I can give you my undivided attention for the next hour." She leaned a fraction closer. "Maybe even settle our bet concerning Dani and Nate."

Heat flared in Aidan's eyes. "Settling the bet will take a few days, at least. But I do know of an abandoned conference room we can use."

Running a hand up his chest and to the back of his neck, she played with his hair. "I am wearing a dress…"

Aidan played with the hem of her skirt. Leaning down to her ear, he whispered, "I see you learned your lesson from last time."

"Well, I've had eleven pairs of jeans ripped in the last ten months because of your impatience."

He nibbled her earlobe. "I seem to recall you ordering me to get them off."

Pressing against his chest, Aidan leaned back to look into her eyes. "Since your memory is so pristine, then you should remember my vow, too, after you ripped the last pair."

"As if that is a punishment. I like chasing you." He released his hold on her and took a step back. "I'll give you a thirty second head start."

Knowing her mate as she did, Claire walked as quickly as she could without drawing attention to herself. The second she hit the hallway, she ran down one of the corridors and then another. She was about to make another turn when strong arms wrapped around her from behind.

Aidan held her against his strong chest. His breath was hot against her cheek. "Got you."

Wiggling her ass, she felt her man's hard cock. "Every second you spend gloating in the hallway is one second less you are inside me."

With a growl, Aidan released her and grabbed her hand. "Forget the conference room." He opened a large storage closet. "We'll do it in here."

Before she could say a word, Aidan picked her up, placed her on top of a few boxes, and shut the door. Kissing his way down her neck, she threaded her fingers through his hair. "You better hope these boxes are sturdy."

He murmured against her skin, "They're boxes of paper. You're fine."

As he gently bit her neck, he ran a hand up her inner thigh. Pushing aside the material of her panties, he teased her opening and growled. "Fuck, Claire, you're so wet. You really do like being chased."

Unashamed, she moved against his hand. "Why are you still talking? The clock is ticking."

He lifted his head. "For that, you're going to pay."

Before she could even frown, Aidan kneeled in front of her, tossed up her skirt, and sliced away her panties. Pushing her legs wide, his eyes glowed amber in the dimly lit closet. "Time to devour your pussy."

No matter how many times he'd said it before, Aidan's words shot straight between her legs. "I'm waiting."

He moved closer and licked her from slit to clit. With a moan, she grabbed onto his head.

Then he took his time licking and sucking, but rarely touching her clit. Only when she growled in frustration and dug her nails into his scalp did he take the hard little nub between his teeth and nibble.

"Aidan."

Swirling the slight sting with his tongue, Claire dropped her head back. She was close.

Another few licks and nibbles, and she screamed. Aidan continued to lick her clit, the sensation prolonging her orgasm.

RESISTING THE COUGAR

When her man finally pulled away, he gave one last lick of his lips. "You're still the best fucking thing I've ever tasted."

Reaching out, she grabbed his shirt and pulled him close. Unzipping his pants, she looked up at him. "Good, then reward me by taking me hard, Aidan. You're behind on my promised number of orgasms."

His cock sprung free and he took it in hand. "It's hard to keep up when there's usually a seven-year-old two bedrooms down the hall."

"Well, we have about forty minutes or so before we need to head back and there aren't any children here. Can you catch up?"

His eyes flashed. With two steps, he was in front of her, his cock teasing her pussy. "You know what you need to say before I start."

"I love you, Aidan Scott."

"And I love you, Claire."

With one swift thrust, he was inside her.

Then he kissed her, his tongue stroking her tongue as he moved his lower body.

Her shifter's taste and scent filled her senses. As his cock pounded in and out of her pussy, Claire took the kiss deeper. Even if she lived to be one hundred, she would never tire of her mate.

Aidan ran one hand down her back and slapped the top of her ass. The slight sting only made her wetter.

As he broke their kiss, his glowing eyes met hers. Both man and beast looked at her like she was the only woman in the world, and her heart warmed. Aidan belonged to her as much as she belonged to him.

After all, shifter mates always belonged to each other.

In the end, Claire was glad she hadn't been able to resist the cougar in front of her. Aidan was everything she never knew she wanted. With him at her side, she could take on the world.

Then her man brushed his fingers against her clit and Claire lost all rational thought as Aidan took her over the edge once more.

Dear Reader:

Thanks for reading *Resisting the Cougar*. I hope you enjoyed Aidan and Claire's story. If you liked their story, please leave a review. Thank you!

The next book will be about Nate and Dani and is called *Charmed by the Bear*. This may be the last book in the series and I hope to have it out in 2017 sometime, if possible. In the meant time, turn the page for the synopsis and an excerpt of *Sacrificed to the Dragon*, the first book my popular Stonefire Dragons series.

To stay up to date on my latest releases, don't forget to sign-up for my newsletter at www.jessiedonovan.com/newsletter.

With Gratitude,
Jessie Donovan

Sacrificed to the Dragon
(Stonefire Dragons #1)

In exchange for a vial of dragon's blood to save her brother's life, Melanie Hall offers herself up as a sacrifice to one of the British dragon-shifter clans. Being a sacrifice means signing a contract to live with the dragon-shifters for six months to try to conceive a child. Her assigned dragonman, however, is anything but easy. He's tall, broody, and alpha to the core. There's only one problem—he hates humans.

Due to human dragon hunters killing his mother, Tristan MacLeod despises humans. Unfortunately, his clan is in desperate need of offspring to repopulate their numbers and it's his turn to service a human female. Despite his plans to have sex with her and walk away, his inner dragon has other ideas. The curvy human female tempts his inner beast like no other.

Excerpt from *Sacrificed to the Dragon*:

CHAPTER ONE

Melanie Hall sat in the reception area of the Manchester Dragon Affairs office, tapping her finger against her arm, and wishing they'd hurry the hell up. She'd been sitting for nearly an hour, and with each minute that ticked by, she started to doubt her eligibility. If she didn't qualify to sacrifice herself to one of the British dragon-shifter clans, her younger brother would die; only the blood of a dragon could cure her brother's antibiotic-resistant CRE infection.

A woman dressed in a gray suit emerged from the far doorway and walked toward her. When she reached Mel, the woman said, "Are you Melanie Hall?" Mel nodded, and the woman turned. "Then follow me."

This is it. Mel rubbed her hands against her black trousers before she stood up and followed the woman. They went down one dull, poorly lit corridor and then turned left to go down another. The woman in the gray suit finally stopped in front of a door that read "Human Sacrifice Liaison" and turned the doorknob. Rather than enter, the middle-aged woman motioned for Mel to go inside. She obeyed, and as soon as she entered the room, the door slammed shut behind her.

A man not much older than her twenty-five years sat at a desk piled high with folders and papers. The room couldn't be bigger than ten feet by ten feet, but it felt even smaller since every available space on the walls was decorated with different maps of the UK. Some were partitioned into five sections, while others had little pins pushed into them. She had no idea what the pins stood for, but the map divided into five represented the five dragon-shifter clans of the United Kingdom—two in England, one in Scotland, one in Northern Ireland, and one in Wales.

One of which might soon be her home for the next six months.

The man cleared his throat and she moved her attention from the walls to his face. When she met his blue eyes, he said, "Take a seat."

Mel sat down in the faded plush chair in front of his desk and waited in silence. She had a tendency to say the wrong thing at the wrong time, and while she usually didn't mind, right now it could end up costing her brother his life.

The man picked up a file folder and scanned something inside with his eyes, and then set it down. She wanted to scream for him to tell her the results, but she bit the inside of her cheek to hold her tongue.

The man's almost bored voice finally filled the room. "Ms. Hall, the genetic testing results say that you are compatible with dragon-shifter DNA and should have no problem conceiving one of their offspring. You also cleared all of the extensive psychological tests. If you're still interested in sacrificing yourself, we can begin the final interview."

Mel blinked. Despite her chances being one in a thousand that she could bear a dragon-shifter child, she qualified. Her younger brother would get the needed dragon's blood and be able to live out a long life free of pain; he now had a future.

Tears pricked her eyes and she closed them to prevent herself from breaking down. *Pull yourself together, Hall.* Crying was the last thing she wanted to do right now. She couldn't give the man any reason to dismiss her as a candidate.

"Ms. Hall?"

Mel opened her eyes and gave a weak smile. "I'm sorry, sir. I'm just relieved that my brother will live."

"Yes, yes, the exchange. But we have a lot to cover before we get to the contract specifics, so if you're quite composed, I'll carry on." Mel sat up straight in her chair and nodded. The man continued. "Right. You are healthy, genetically compatible, fertile, unattached, and not a virgin, which are the five requirements needed to qualify. Sacrificing yourself means that you will go to live with Clan Stonefire for a period of six months, and be assigned a temporary male. You will consent to his sexual attentions, and if you become pregnant, you understand that your stay will be extended until after the child is born. If you have any questions, any at all, now is the time to ask them."

She had heard the basics before, but now that she'd passed all of the tests, panic squeezed her heart. As much as she wanted to save her brother—and she would save him—being assigned to have sex with an unknown male dragon-shifter was more than a little scary. Especially since many human women died in the process of birthing half dragon-shifter babies.

If the death-by-baby aspect wasn't bad enough, she was putting her life on hold to do this. Mel was one thesis away from earning her PhD in Social Anthropology. If she became pregnant and survived the delivery, she wasn't sure she could just give up the child and walk away. Most of the women sacrifices who lived past the delivery did abandon their children, but no matter how different the dragon-shifters were from humans, Mel wouldn't be one of them. Family meant everything to her.

And if she didn't give up her child, she would have to give up her dreams in order to spend the rest of her life with Clan Stonefire.

She took a deep breath and remembered her brother Oliver, pale and thin in his sickbed, and her worry dissipated to a manageable level. Even if she became a mother before she'd planned, she would do it three times over to give Oliver a chance to see past his fifteenth birthday.

Still, she wasn't about to pass up this opportunity to ask some questions. The dragon-shifters were extremely private, rarely sharing anything that happened on their land with the public. "I understand consenting to sexual activity, as my main purpose is to help repopulate the dragon-shifters, but what guarantees are in place to ensure I'm not abused or neglected?"

The man leaned back in his chair and steepled his fingers in front of him. "I understand your concern, but the UK Department of Dragon Affairs conducts routine inspections and interviews. Childbearing-related mortality aside, over the last ten years, only one sacrifice has ever reported harsh treatment out of hundreds."

With colossal effort, she managed not to think about her fifty-fifty chance of surviving childbirth. "And what about my friends and family? Can I communicate with them?"

"Communication is forbidden for the first six weeks. After that, it is entirely up to your assigned male as to whether you can communicate or not. From experience, the women who made the greatest effort to conceive were awarded the most privileges."

Right. So if she became a sex goddess, she could talk with her family. How she was going to accomplish that since her previous boyfriends had told her she was "good enough" but never fantastic, she had no idea. But she would cross that bridge when she came to it. "And lastly, when will my brother receive his treatment and when will I leave for the dragons' compound?"

"Once our legal representative has gone through the contract with you and it's been signed and witnessed, a copy will be sent to Clan Stonefire. They should approve it within a matter of days and deliver the vial of dragon's blood to your brother's physician. Normally, you'd be expected to arrive within a week. However, in the case of dying relatives, you're given two weeks to set your affairs in order and to be assured that your brother is recovering. Our office will notify you of the particulars within the next five days."

The man picked up a pen and signed something inside the manila folder on his desk. He picked up a piece of paper and held it out to her. "Since you've had a rational conversation without breaking down or bursting into tears, I think you're mentally sound enough to be sacrificed. If you have no further questions, you can proceed to the legal department."

Even at this late stage of the application process, she now understood how some candidates might be scared off. Hearing about no communication with the outside world as well as how giving birth to a half-dragon baby might kill you was a lot to take in. But Melanie wasn't doing this for herself. Oliver had had a shitty last few years fighting off cancer only to beat it and end up with a drug-resistant infection that was slowly killing him.

Her funny, clever brother deserved a chance to live and enjoy life.

She reached out and took the paper. She said, "Thank you. I'm still interested. Please tell me where the legal department is located, and I'll go there straightaway."

He gave her the directions. Mel thanked the man before leaving his office and making the necessary turns. As she approached the last turn, she glanced down at the paper in her hands. Toward the bottom of the sheet, the man had checked "approved" and signed his name. Seeing it in black and white made her stomach flip.

In less than two weeks, she would go to live with the dragon-shifters and be expected to have sex with one of their males.

She took a deep breath and pushed back the sense of panic. While she didn't know how her assigned dragonman would treat her, there was one thing she had to look forward to—the men were rumored to be fit and muscled. For once in her life, Melanie would get to sleep with a strong, hot man. She only hoped he wouldn't be a complete bastard.

~~~

Tristan MacLeod knocked on the cottage door of Stonefire's clan leader. When he heard a muffled, "Come in," he twisted the knob and entered.

Bram Moore-Llewellyn, Stonefire's clan leader and Tristan's friend of nearly thirty years, sat behind the old, sturdy oak desk that had been used by leaders of the clan for over a hundred years. It was beat up with more than a few scratches from young dragon-shifters trying out their talons. Tristan thought it looked like shit, but dragons were big on tradition and Stonefire's clan leader was no exception.

Bram motioned for Tristan to come in and sit in one of the wooden chairs in front of his desk. Shutting the door, Tristan complied.

While he had a feeling he knew what this meeting was about, he asked, "You wanted to see me?"

Bram put aside the papers he'd been reading and looked up at him. "It's time, Tristan."

Fuck. "Can't one of the volunteer males have another turn? Putting me together with a human is a bad idea, Bram, and you know it."

Bram leaned back in his chair and shook his head. "No. I can't risk the gene pool getting too small. Neither you nor your sister has had any young, and since you're the elder, you're first in line. I hate to be a hardass, but if you refuse to pair with the latest human sacrifice, I'll have to kick you out of the clan."

Want to read the rest?
Sacrificed to the Dragon is available in paperback

For exclusive content and updates, sign up for my newsletter at:

http://www.jessiedonovan.com

AUTHOR'S NOTE

I enjoyed revisiting the world of the Cascade Shifters. I'm excited to write Nate and Dani's story, although I have a feeling I won't have a chance to write it until next year some time. (Yes, my publishing schedule is that full!) Still, I hope you'll continue to follow the series as I write it. You can join my newsletter at jessiedonovan.com to keep in touch.

As always, I have a few people to thank:

- Becky Johnson of Hot Tree Editing is amazing. I'm very fortunate to have her as my editor. Because of her, I'm a much stronger writer.
- My team of betas—Iliana, Donna, and Alyson— take their valuable time to comment and help with typos. They also make me a better writer. For this book, Iliana really pushed me to be better and I thank her.
- My cover artist, Clarissa of Yocla Designs, is outstanding as always. Each new cover she creates is my new favorite. I honestly don't think I could choose just one!

And lastly, I thank you, the reader. Without you, I wouldn't be able to write stories for a living. Thanks for your support, word of mouth, and encouragement. It means the world to me!

ABOUT THE AUTHOR

Jessie Donovan wrote her first story at age five, and after discovering *The Dragonriders of Pern* series by Anne McCaffrey in junior high, she realized people actually wanted to read stories like those floating around inside her head. From there on out, she was determined to tap into her over-active imagination and write a book someday.

After living abroad for five years and earning degrees in Japanese, Anthropology, and Secondary Education, she buckled down and finally wrote her first full-length book. While that story will never see the light of day, it laid the world-building groundwork of what would become her debut paranormal romance, *Blaze of Secrets*. In late 2014 she officially became a *New York Times* and *USA Today* bestselling author.

Jessie loves to interact with readers, and when not reading a book or traipsing around some foreign country on a shoestring, can often be found on Facebook:

http://www.facebook.com/JessieDonovanAuthor

And don't forget to sign-up for her newsletter to receive sneak peeks and inside information. You can sign-up on her website:

http:///www.jessiedonovan.com